Morning
is
Dead

Andersen Prunty

GRINDHOUSE PRESS

Published by Grindhouse Press
grindhousepress@yahoo.com

Morning is Dead
ISBN-13: 978-0-9826281-0-2
ISBN-10: 09826281

This book is a work of fiction.

Morning
is
Dead

"And then he thought he saw a man walking along the edge of the little wood. In great strides, as if he didn't want night to overtake him. He wondered who the man was. The only way he could tell it was a man and not a shadow was because he wore a shirt and swung his arms as he walked."
    Roberto Bolaño, *2666*

A Hospital at Night
Part One

The steady beep in her right ear held April in a state of near hypnosis. Did she want it to continue beeping steadily or just stop altogether? The lights were off. Alvin lay in front of her, eyes closed, wrapped in gauze, tubes snaking out from his nose and mouth—feeding him, making him breathe, keeping him alive. She cradled her bandaged right arm in her lap, looked past the bed, through the darkness of the hospital room, at her vague reflection in the glass of the darkened window. Tears glistened on her cheeks. She breathed in a wet and snotty breath and sat back in the uncomfortable chair. She didn't think she deserved comfort.

A gentle hand pressed down on her shoulder. She was too numb to be startled.

"He's gone." Mirabel placed her other hand on her other shoulder.

April was momentarily confused. Who was gone? Alvin wasn't gone. The beeping told her he was still alive.

"I'm sorry," Mirabel said.

Morning. She was talking about Morning. Brett Morning. "Brett" to April. "Dr. Morning" to Mirabel and the rest of the hospital's employees and April when she was on the clock.

"When?" The mucous in April's mouth had thickened. The tears came harder. She would have thought she had been saving it all up but it seemed like she did nothing but cry these past few months.

"He was dead when the ambulance brought him in."

April shook her head. This was all her fault. Take her out of the equation and no one was dead. No one was dying. No one was being kept alive by tubes and beeping and the chilly sterility of an anonymous hospital room.

Mirabel slid a chair over beside April. She hadn't even felt her hands leave her shoulders.

Mirabel sat down, placing a comforting hand on April's thigh. "Wanna talk about it? I mean, I imagine you're going to have to talk to the police anyway but, you know, wanna tell someone who'll care?"

April nodded. She didn't know if she *could* talk. "It's a mess."

"Honey, I think that's a bit of an understatement. But there wasn't a mess that couldn't be cleaned up."

April held her wrapped arm up to her eyes and let the gauze absorb the tears. She wondered if she would have a scar and knew she would and felt bad for thinking vain thoughts at a time like this.

"Were you and Morning…?"

"Together?"

"Yeah."

"For the past few months."

"I had no idea."

"We did a good job of keeping it a secret."

"Not from everyone." Mirabel nodded toward Alvin.

"He was so messed up. I didn't think he would notice, let alone care. Now they're both gone."

"He's not gone yet."

"Banks said he wouldn't be out of the woods until dawn. He said it was unlikely he'd last until then."

"Go on," Mirabel said. "Talk it out."

"I didn't know he had problems when we got married. Maybe he didn't. He never even acted very weird. But I'd find the shit all over the house... I started to notice the marks on his arms. He came back a couple of weeks ago and found the door unlocked. He acted like nothing was different, even though I didn't know where he'd been for nearly a month before that, and he hadn't really *been* there for at least three months. I... locked him out. Called the police. That was the last time I saw him before tonight. It wasn't just the drugs. He had mental problems. I tried to have him committed but he would just check himself out a few days later."

One

Alvin Blue stood on his back porch. He took a deep breath of the late September night air. It was dark and the neighborhood was asleep. It seemed like the neighborhood was always asleep. Traffic picked up at the beginning and end of the school day and when the bars closed around 2:30. But it was all just people racing to their houses. Rushing their children indoors to the controlled climate and television.

He didn't know any of his neighbors' names.

Sometimes he lifted his hand in a poor excuse for a wave but only if one of them had caught him staring. They never waved back. Just looked at the ground and walked quicker. Maybe pretended to cough in order to feign some preoccupation.

He looked around at his yard. It needed mowing. No time like the present. If anyone decided to complain about the noise he would relish the confrontation. The interaction.

Reaching his hand into the pocket of his old blue jeans, he closed it around the key to the utility shed and strolled out into the yard. He opened the shed and pulled out the lawnmower, a cheap green push model. He bent down and pressed the rubbery red button a few times to prime the engine. Then engaged the clutch against the handle, grabbed the starter cord, and gave it a yank. The mower roared into life.

He mowed the grass quickly and furiously, following the same exact pattern he had for the past five years. The street lamps provided enough light. It took him about a half hour. He broke a sweat and developed a great thirst.

He put the lawnmower away and locked the shed. He looked around the neighborhood. Their house sat on a corner lot facing Angler Street. Roughly a quarter mile long, Angler ran east to west, ending in an alley to the east and Thistle Street to the west. Thistle ran north to south and ended at Payne, a busy four-lane avenue that ran all the way downtown.

Where were the angry neighbors?

He didn't even see lights on in any of the houses. Coma city.

He went inside to the refrigerator and grabbed a beer. He twisted off the bottle cap, tossed it toward the trashcan, missed, and left it there on the floor. He looked at the bottle. He usually drank Guinness. This was a Heineken. When had he bought that?

"Al?"

It was April, wandering downstairs. She stepped around the refrigerator, rubbing her eyes against the light. She wore a tight yellow t-shirt and white underwear. Five years of marriage hadn't touched her. She looked as good as the day he'd met her. Better, probably.

"Yeah?" He raised his beer and took a healthy swig.

"Were you mowing the grass?"

"Yeah. It needed done."

"It's late." She turned to look behind her.

"I know. I didn't figure anyone would care."

"Woke *me* up."

"Sorry."

"Coming to bed soon?" She had her cell phone in her hand. She had become so paranoid.

"In a bit. After I drink this."

"Just one?"

"Maybe two or three."

"Or six?"

"Not enough time."

"And that's all you're gonna do? Just drink a few beers?"

"Yeah. What else would I do?"

"You shouldn't stay up so late."

"I know. I'll come to bed in a bit."

He closed the distance between them and bent to kiss her. She blocked him with her hand. "I've been asleep. My breath is horrible."

He pecked her on the top of the head.

"Night," he said, rubbing his hands through her short blond hair.

"Night."

She turned toward the living room. He listened to her footsteps fade up the stairs. She talked to herself as she went. He grabbed the rest of the six pack from the fridge. There were three other bottles in there. He opened the doors beneath the sink and reached into the little hole in the bottom of the cabinetry where one of the pipes ran down through the floor. He extracted a hidden pack of cigarettes and went back out to the porch. The neighborhood was still dead but, to him, the air was alive with the smell of fresh cut grass, the earliest hint of fall, and the hoppy scent of beer. He put a cigarette in his mouth and blazed up. He'd waited all day for this.

He sat down on one of the deck chairs, imitation wicker strung across cast iron, and put his feet up on the other chair. He smoked his cigarette, drank his beer, and listened to all the distant sounds—bottles emptying from the bar one street over, sirens, trains, airplanes overhead.

A half hour passed. Three beers and six cigarettes later, he felt a tingling glow throughout his body. And deep in the glow, he felt the anger. This was perfection. If everything could be like this moment, then life would be perfect. But it wasn't. He'd lost his job at the Point. He hadn't told April yet. He wondered if she knew. She hadn't said anything if she did. He pretended to go to work. First he drove and then decided he was just wasting money on gas. So he sold the car and told April he was taking the bus. His days were foggy. A lot of things were foggy. And then other things, like now, like here, like sitting on the back porch in the crisp night air, were crystal clear. So clear they gleamed and shined and hummed through his bones.

He saw a man carrying a bow enter the alley behind the house.

This movement in an area of typical stillness was disconcerting.

The archer wore camouflage coveralls and a rotund pack on his back, a quiver of arrows jutting above his right shoulder.

Alvin's heart thudded. Sped up. Blood rushed to his head and his ears rang. Then he noticed the archer didn't have his sight on him. Still, he rose slowly, only a little wobbly from the beer. Beer never used to make him feel like this.

The archer moved stealthily. A large rabbit sat in the shadows at the end of Alvin's lawn.

Alvin reached back and put his hand on the handle of the storm door. One could not be too cautious.

The archer raised his bow, slow and smooth, without making a sound. Alvin could just as well have been watching something on a muted television. The archer pulled back the bowstring and held it for just a second before letting go. The arrow moved so quickly, Alvin didn't even see it. He heard a *thunk* and a small cry. Did rabbits even make sounds? He didn't think they did. Not normally, anyway. He looked toward the end of his lawn at the rabbit squirming furiously, the arrow pinning it to the ground. The archer didn't seem to take any notice of him and Alvin thought that was probably just as well. The archer reached into his pocket, pulled out a knife and flipped it open. He approached the rabbit, crouched down, put his free hand around the back of its neck and slit its throat.

Alvin wanted to throw a beer bottle at him but thought, in the end, he might find himself outmatched. What could he do? It seemed like he should do something. Call the police? No. It probably wasn't worth it and, who knew, maybe the archer was just some homeless guy who needed the rabbit for food. The archer wiped his knife in the grass, removed the arrow and wiped that in the grass before replacing it in his quiver. He lifted the rabbit up and pressed his mouth to the underside of its neck.

Jesus, Alvin thought, he's drinking its blood.

The archer kept the rabbit pressed to his mouth for nearly a minute before pulling it away and deftly opening his pack while it was still on his back. Then he stuffed the rabbit in and continued further into the alley.

Alvin cautiously crept down to the end of his lawn. The archer was about midway down the alley. He turned and shouted, "These are rock hard times, friend!" before turning and continuing on his way.

Alvin went back up to the porch and lit another cigarette. He needed it after that. Once finished, he chucked it out into the yard and hoped sleep would come quickly. He pulled the storm door open and turned the knob on the door.

Shit. It was locked.

He didn't remember locking it. In fact, he usually took precautions to make sure it was never locked.

Oh well. He still had his keys in his pocket.

He reached his hand in. No keys. He definitely didn't remember taking them out of his pocket. He didn't have any reason to. He checked his other pocket to make sure his cell phone wasn't in there. It wasn't. He would have to beat on the door until April heard him.

Just as he started to really lay into it, he saw movement in the kitchen. The light was on. He hoped it was April's shadow from the living room. Maybe she had had some kind of psychic calling or something.

No.

He didn't see her.

But there was still that shadowy movement. Maybe it was a reflection. He could even make out a face. There. On the other side of the glass. It kind of looked like him. Only it didn't. Not really. The face was too sculptured and pale. Alvin blinked his eyes. Took a step back.

There was someone in the house.

9

Crazy panic shot through his body.

A man was in the house. A man who looked kind of like him only better. And he was better dressed than Alvin, wearing a well-cut dark suit. He didn't look like a maniac but why would he be in the house?

The man made eye contact with Alvin.

Then he raised the index finger of his right hand and drew it across his throat. The gesture was childish and endlessly threatening.

Alvin wasn't going to let this happen. He played with the pneumatic catch at the top of the storm door to prop it open. He grabbed one of the deck chairs and slammed it against the glass of the door. A crack opened in one of the panes. The man stood just on the other side of the glass, unflinching.

Alvin brought the chair back for another go when an amplified voice from behind him said, "Please put the chair down!"

He turned to see a police car, lights flashing, in the alleyway.

Good, he thought. Someone who could help him.

A Hospital at Night
Part Two

Another volley of tears shuddered through April. She bent forward. Mirabel rubbed her back.

"I just can't believe he's gone. You don't think it's awful... that I wasn't there with him, do you? I just couldn't see him like that."

"It's okay, honey. Did he have anyone else?"

"Do you mean was *he* married, too?"

Mirabel patted her on the good arm, took her hand and held it with her own.

"No. Thank god. Alvin started seeing things, Mir. He would talk about conversations that didn't happen. A lot of times I *knew* because I was standing right there when he allegedly had them. He was a stranger. I didn't know what to think. That's what it's like when you think you know somebody so well and then realize you never knew him at all. I was scared. So I started letting Brett stay over. I shouldn't have done that. I should have stayed at his place but I thought... I thought if Alvin had the house to himself he wouldn't last a week. This way I could kind of keep an eye on him."

Two

Alvin placed the chair back on the porch and descended the steps to meet the approaching police officer. The officer didn't look at all like a cop. His hair flowed down to the middle of his back, his shirt was untucked, he was very thin, and he wobbled when he walked. He held a cell phone up to his left ear.

"Well, I gotta go. I gotta make an arrest. Huh? Oh, I don't know. Some asshole. Yeah, I got some stuff. Later. Bye."

Alvin, less than two feet away, stared at the cop.

The cop flipped his phone shut and stuck it in his pants pocket. He looked at Alvin with heavy-lidded, bloodshot eyes.

"I don't think there will be any need to make an arrest, sir," Alvin said.

"I didn't just drive out here for nothing."

"I think it's just a misunderstanding. Someone broke into my house. That's the person you should be arresting. My wife is in there sleeping." Alvin pointed over his shoulder, hoping the strange man was staring out the window, hoping to catch his arrest.

"No one broke into your home. What are you doing outside?"

"Trying to get back in."

"Sounds like you're the one trying to break into a home."

"It's *my* home."

"Are you the one who called?"

"No. I left my phone inside."

"Uh-huh."

"Look, Officer..." Alvin studied the man's nametag. "Fuckpants?"

"Yeah, I'm Officer Fuckpants." His lips twitched with suppressed laughter as he spoke.

"I locked myself outside and when I tried to get back in I saw a man in the kitchen."

"Maybe because he's the one who lives here."

"No, he doesn't. I live here."

"Is it that guy?"

Fuckpants pointed to the house. Alvin saw the man in the glow of the kitchen, staring out.

"Yeah."

"Yeah. He's staying here. I'm sorry but I'm gonna have to take you in. Don't make this end up in a restraining order."

"What? Why are you taking me in?"

"Breaking and entering. Disturbing the peace." The cop leaned in and sniffed. "Public intoxication. You're wiped out, man. Let me take you in and you can get a little rest. Get your head cleared."

"Ludicrous."

"Follow me."

Alvin thought about protesting and saw his list of

charges escalate: resisting arrest, assaulting a police officer.

"It's okay to be upset. Nobody likes to get arrested."

Was this guy even a cop?

"I need to see a badge," Alvin said. "I'm not going anywhere until I see a badge."

"Gimme a fuckin' break." Fuckpants reached into his back pocket and pulled out a beaded hemp wallet. He flipped it open and stuck the badge less than an inch in front of Alvin's face. "There ya go. That badgy enough for ya?"

Alvin had no idea what a real badge looked like. It looked like it was made out of metal, not plastic. Was that good enough? He didn't know. Probably didn't have much of a choice.

"Come on." Fuckpants began walking toward the squad car, pulled half up onto the curb like he had arrived during some great emergency. "You'll have to get in on the passenger side. Backseat's full."

Alvin glanced into the backseat. A fat man in a white t-shirt lay sprawled across it, either deeply asleep or dead.

"I guess I should put these on you." Fuckpants pulled out a pair of handcuffs. "Put your hands behind your back."

"Honestly."

"When I show up to the scene of a crime and some crazy fucker's tryin' to break out a window, I become concerned for my personal safety. I'm sorry if you don't see that as an issue."

Alvin turned around, pressing himself against the car, and held his arms behind him. "Aren't you going to read me my rights or anything?"

"You don't have any."

The cold cuffs encircled his wrists.

"That's too tight."

The cop chuffed out a breath. "You're lucky they ain't cobras. That's how they do it some places. Wrap a couple cobras around your wrists for cuffs. That's some scary terrorist torture shit, you ask me."

Fuckpants closed his hand around Alvin's left arm and guided him to the passenger side of the car. He opened it and crammed Alvin in.

Alvin stared back at his house. There were people on the roof. About six of them. They wore black coveralls and gas masks. He squinted at the lettering on their backs. Acme Demolition. They dropped things that looked like thick wires off the roof: red and yellow and green.

The cop opened the driver's side door and hopped in.

"What are those people doing on top of the house?" Alvin asked.

The cop looked back at the house. "Looks like they're wirin' it up."

"Wiring it up? Why?"

"I don't know. Maybe it's scheduled."

"Scheduled?"

"For detonation. They've been doin' it to a lot of the houses in the area. Looks like they're just gettin' started. Probably has three days, tops." Fuckpants fired up the ignition. Led Zeppelin blasted out of the speakers. The cop pulled away from the curb and proceeded to sing along with the song, mimicking Robert Plant's high-pitched voice. Alvin leaned over and placed his forehead against the cool glass as they pulled out onto Payne and made a right, going toward downtown.

A Hospital at Night
Part Three

Beep. Beep. Beep.

April couldn't figure out if the sound was comforting or something like a death knell.

"Sometimes he would just get mad at everyone and rant for what felt like hours. He said everyone was asleep. No one could do anything right. Sometimes, in public, he would point to someone, and say that person was asleep. He said he wished the sleepers wouldn't feel the need to walk around and act awake. He said he wished they would just stay asleep. Everything was some kind of conspiracy. He said they were really supposed to be sleeping and were only awakened so they could consume things. He said if you just stripped away everything from these people— television and movies and malls and restaurants and cars and everything it is that it seems like most people work for—that they would just curl up and go back to sleep and sleep forever. He wondered if they dreamed. He said they were dead inside."

Three

They cruised down Payne Avenue. The Point, the place where Alvin used to work, loomed on the hill just beyond the city, surrounded by a noxious looking greenish brown luminescence. Jets of orange fire shot up from the gloom. This far away, you couldn't hear it. But, Alvin knew, the closer you got, the louder it was. Inside was a constant, deafening roar that bludgeoned its way through your skin and got into your viscera and bones and ricocheted around until you could feel your brain rattling against your skull.

It was like the Point sucked all the energy out of the city. It gave people a place to work and it paid them decently but it also told them they were little more than pieces of a machine. Not just the actual machinery of the Point but the machinery of society as well. The workers at the Point made money and took out mortgages and car payments and consumed everything they could get their hands on until they were overweight, abusive, alcoholic basket cases. This was normal. This was normal. This was normal.

Alvin wondered about that. He didn't think there was anything normal about it.

The city was rife with sores and blights and rot. Alvin noticed several of the houses and buildings that must have been detonated. He could have asked Fuckpants about it but the music was way too loud. Sandwiched in between two perfectly fine houses with lights in at least one of the windows would be a blackened husk. Or a pile of rubble.

The cars parked on the sides of the road were rusted, multicolor hulks. The people walking along the sidewalks were skeletal, all their clothes stained a dingy, uniform color very much like the grainy darkness around them.

Alvin hadn't noticed any of this before.

Fuckpants pulled a cigarette from his breast pocket and lit it. He sucked in deeply and Alvin realized the cop was smoking marijuana. He held it down as long as he could, grunting with the effort. He exhaled a plume of smoke and unleashed a volley of coughs. He proffered the joint to Alvin who shook his head.

"You're a straight, huh?" Fuckpants asked him.

"It's illegal. I don't want to be in any more trouble than I already am." He had to talk loud over the music. He hated classic rock. He'd heard all the songs a million times when he was in high school and didn't have a particular desire to listen to them again.

"Shit," Fuckpants said. "There's worse things than a little weed."

"I can't believe you're really a cop."

"Well, I'm more of a night cop. We're a different breed. See that fellow sleepin' back there? He's a daytime cop. He's been out for quite a while. I ain't seen the sun in... Jesus, I don't know how long it's been."

How long had it been since *Alvin* had seen daylight? He couldn't remember. There was the period when he pretended to go to work but… things got hazy after that. Maybe he slept all day. He was tired a lot. The last time he was awake during the day he remembered thinking the brightness of it was harsh and oppressive. He had just wanted to be inside somewhere, anywhere, draw the blinds, and wait for night to come. Maybe that was what he needed. A night shift job. Maybe he could get hired back on at the Point for third shift work.

The cop took another toke off the joint. He slung his head around and sang along with the music. Alvin wondered exactly how high the cop was. A light in front of them turned red and Fuckpants stopped the car about twenty feet in front of it. He took another drag off the joint.

This can't be real, Alvin thought. He needed to get back to April. This cop was just playing games. He hadn't done anything illegal. And April could be in serious trouble. Who was that man in there with her? He kind of looked like Alvin but Alvin didn't think April would believe it was him. He could be a rapist. He could be a murderer. And the cop had seen him but now Alvin was the one going to jail. It didn't make any sense. And what about those people wiring up the house? What if they detonated it while she was still in there?

The light turned green and Fuckpants stepped slowly onto the accelerator. Alvin began thrashing in the passenger seat, throwing his shoulder against the door.

Fuckpants looked over at him. "Whoa," he said. "Whoa now. Take it easy."

Alvin clenched his teeth, rocked vigorously forward and back, banging into the seat with all of his weight. "Let me out! Let me out! Let me out!"

Fuckpants slammed on the brakes and the car went sliding sideways. He angrily roached his joint in the ashtray, sparks flickering lazily to the floor. "Now listen here," he said, his bloodshot eyes gone wild and crazy. "You ain't goin' nowhere. You're goin' to the station with me. You were implicated in a very serious crime and we can't let that go unpunished. Besides, you need to be processed."

"Processed! What the fuck do you mean?! You're a fucking lunatic! This whole thing is madness! Turn! Down! The! Fucking! Radio!" Alvin rammed his knee against what he thought was the radio. There were so many electronic gadgets in the dash, he didn't know what was what.

Fuckpants angrily poked at a bunch of buttons until the radio fell silent. Then he brought back his right hand and punched Alvin in the face. Blood trickled from his nose. He licked it away from his upper lip and spat at the cop. "My wife is in my home with a complete stranger who is posing as me. I was only trying to get back into my house. I'm sure you have some sort of database you can look in to see that it *is* my home. You can see my driver's license to verify that."

Fuckpants just shook his head. "It ain't nearly that easy. You've entered into a whole fuck lot of red tape. You probably won't be back home for weeks, at least. I think it's time you faced reality and admit to yourself your little wife's found a new fuck buddy."

"You're an asshole."

"Be that as it may, I'm also an officer of the law. And you have broken the law. And you will be punished."

He backed the car up and hit the accelerator. The car went shooting down the avenue once again. Now they were going downhill, only a few minutes away from downtown. At the next light, a man was crossing the street. It looked like he was glowing. It looked like he was green. Alvin felt his foot pressing an imaginary brake on the floorboard. But Fuckpants seemed unconcerned. Alvin's heart rate slowed a little when it looked like the glowing man was going to make it to the next lane without being hit. Then Fuckpants swerved over to hit him head on. The car smashed into him with a meaty impact and just kept going. Alvin turned to look at the man splattered and twisted on the road. Turning back to stare at the windshield, he saw a glowing neon green substance slathered all over it. Fuckpants turned on the windshield washer and wipers until it was mostly gone.

Before Alvin could say anything, Fuckpants said, "Don't worry about it, it was just a raid."

"A raid?"

"Rade. R-A-D-E. It's short for radiation victim. No one really knows what they are but most people think they come from the Point."

"I worked there and I've never seen anything like that. I don't even think the Point deals in radiation."

"Oh, the Point wouldn't acknowledge that they had anything to do with it. The bigwigs there have everybody convinced the rades are public nuisance number one."

"I've never even heard of them."

"You wouldn't unless you come out at night a lot."

"I can't remember the last time I was out during the *day*."

"The night has a lot more levels than the day. You'll find out after you've been processed."

"What the fuck is wrong with you? I don't need to get processed. I need to get home."

"You can forget about that. I'm going to take you back to the station and you're going to be processed. Processed deeper into the night."

Alvin didn't know if Fuckpants was serious or just trying to scare him. "You're a fucking halfwit."

"Keep it up with that smart mouth. Your list of crimes just keeps gettin' longer and longer. Wanna know why the rades are considered a nuisance?"

"Why not."

"Let me ask you this, first of all, what did you do at the Point?"

"I worked in human resources, data entry kind of stuff mostly."

"Oh, so you worked in an *office*?"

"Mostly, but I started out in the foundry just like everybody else."

"So I guess you think that makes you better than the rest of 'em? 'Cause you was able to work your way up?"

"No, not at all. I'm just... I just wasn't cut out for the foundry. What does this have to do with anything?"

"Well, I was just wonderin' how come you never heard about the rades and now I know; it's 'cause you weren't down there with everybody else. Now, this's been a recent phenomenon. They say one of the workers was exposed to so much toxic shit he started to turn green and shit and then, get this, he started to develop *needles* growin' outta his fingertips. Lost all his hair. Couldn't wear clothes 'cause they'd just burn up when they touched that skin. Then his dick fell off. The fucker wasn't even human no more. Then he started stickin' those needles into other folks and they started turnin' into things just like him. Now it ain't illegal to kill 'em or nothin'. Fact, it's encouraged. 'Cause once you turn into a rade, there ain't no turnin' back."

Alvin just shook his head. If his hands were not cuffed behind him, he would have closed them over his ears so he didn't have to listen to Fuckpants anymore.

"Fine. Don't believe me." He reached into the ashtray and fished out his joint. He lit it up again, flaming sparks drifting down to his shirt, and took a deep breath. "Once you get deeper into the night you're gonna see a whole bunch of shit."

Alvin leaned forward and put his head on the dashboard. "Fucking kill me now."

"No time soon!" Fuckpants shouted and hit the stereo button again. This time it was Rush. Alvin fought the urge to throw up.

A Hospital at Night
Part Four

April hadn't said anything for some time. She sat with her elbows in her lap, her hands covering her eyes, shuddering and crying and trying to breathe steadily.

"How's the arm feeling?" Mirabel asked.

"I think I need to use the restroom."

April shakily stood and walked to the bathroom at the corner of the room. She flipped on the light. It was white, fluorescent, and stinging. She had the vague sense it had torn something apart. She shut the door and didn't bother to lock it. She lifted the crescent seat of the toilet, dropped to her knees, and vomited into it, black swirling with clear mucous. She had a desire to reach into the bowl and grab the vomit and lift it out by the handful and put it back in her mouth. She was tired of losing parts of herself.

Mirabel tapped gently on the door. "You okay, honey?"

April put the seat back down with a pristine plastic clapping sound.

"I'm okay. I'll be out in just a second."

She turned the faucet to the sink on and splashed some cold water in her face. She refused to look directly at the mirror. She patted her face dry with a hand towel, opened the door, and turned off the light. Mirabel was there, putting a heavy arm around her shoulders, guiding her back to the chair.

She sat down and stared at Alvin and his tubes. She didn't know what to feel. Pity. Anger. Sadness. Love. Hate. Maybe it was all the same in the end.

"Morning's dead. Does that make you feel better? Does that make you happy?"

"Now now." Mirabel patted her good arm. "That's not gonna do anybody any good."

Now April clutched Mirabel's hand and gave it a little shake. "I might need a minute to be alone."

Mirabel stood up and ran a hand along the top of April's head. "I should probably be doing my rounds anyway. Give Jackie a chance to go have a cigarette. You gonna be okay?"

"You'll come back?"

"As soon as I can."

"I'll be fine."

"You need anything, you know how to get me here. You need anything before I go?"

"I'm okay."

Mirabel turned to leave and then stopped. She spoke to April's back. "This isn't gonna end here tonight, you know. Regardless of what happens with Alvin, you're gonna need someone to talk to after you get home and maybe for a long time to come. I'll always listen. I just want you to know that."

April nodded so Mirabel could see she understood because, of all the people who could have said this to April, she knew Mirabel was the only one who meant it.

Morning is Dead

Mirabel's shoes squeaked away and then April was left with the relative silence of the room.

The beeping from the machines.

The dry hiss of the breathing apparatus.

The same sounds from a dozen other rooms.

The hushed conversations of the night shift.

The distant sound of a train.

The clanking from a warehouse next to the hospital.

The wind howling through the trees.

The clouds billowing in on themselves.

The insectoid drone of the moon.

The clicking of the stars.

The cold crackle of space.

Silence wasn't really silent at all.

Four

Fuckpants ran the car up onto the curb in front of the police station. Alvin's head smacked into the passenger side window and he barked out in pain. He thought the joint would have mellowed Fuckpants out but it seemed to have sent him into a furor. Or maybe Alvin had sent him into a furor. Fuckpants threw open the driver's side door, not bothering to turn off the car, went around to the passenger side, and dragged Alvin out. He grabbed him around the right arm and marched him up the steps leading to the station. He threw open the doors, walked Alvin to a chair, and sat him down.

"I gotta go cool off," he said to an officer sitting at the desk across from Alvin. Fuckpants stormed into an office off the main area and slammed the door. Reggae music soon wafted out from behind it.

Looking around the police station made Alvin think of an opium den. The officers were sitting at desks or on brightly colored beanbags. None of them looked older than twenty-five. A cloud of smoke had collected at the ceiling and the whole place was redolent with marijuana, opium, and quite possibly crack. One officer sat at his desk reading a Nietzsche book and taking slugs from a bottle of Jack Daniel's. A male officer and what may have been a prostitute made out on a desk to Alvin's left. The officer across the desk from him had his sleeve rolled up and slid a needle out of his arm before unstrapping the tubing and holding the syringe out to Alvin.

"Want some?"

"I don't think so," Alvin said.

"Very well." The officer's eyes threatened to close, his head bobbing forward. "Then."

He put the syringe in a drawer and held out his hand. He spoke very slowly. "I'm sorry to see you... here."

Jesus, Alvin thought. This guy's threatening to nod off.

"I suppose you've come to be... processed?"

"Let me try and reason with you, Officer... Bitchhole?"

"That's right." He tried to smile but his pale face wasn't working very well.

"I don't know why I'm here. My wife is at home with a strange man in the house. He could be doing God knows what to her and I'm stuck in this lunacy."

"Not lunacy. The law."

"Whatever. I need to get home to her. I would ask you to send an officer there but you all seem pretty incapacitated."

"We have a... good time."

"I need to go."

Alvin stood up to head for the door. A gunshot rang out and splintered the jamb to his right. His ears rang loudly. He turned back around to see Bitchhole trying to hold the gun. He probably could have just left but figured if Bitchhole tried to wing him he might end up shooting him in the head instead.

"I'm afraid... you won't be able to go for... long time."
He thunked the gun back down on the wooden desk. It dis-
charged again and took out a window. "You need...
processed." He swiveled in his chair and pointed with an
arm gone floppy and limp. "Go down that hall on... left."

Alvin crossed the room. The makeout couple on his left
had now graduated to open sex. The cop had the woman's
skirt up around her waist, bending her over the desk. His
hips moved slowly, buttocks pale under the harsh fluorescent station lights. "Need any help finding it?" he asked
casually.

"No. I think I can manage. You look busy anyway."

"Fuck yeah."

The woman moaned in ecstasy. They were probably *on*
ecstasy.

Alvin continued walking toward the barred back wall of
the station. Three cells lined the wall. Two of them were
occupied by what looked like a sleeping homeless guy and
a very intense wiry man wearing a mint green outfit made
from bath towels. Alvin started down the hallway. It was
long and dark. There were no doors lining it. Like it was
designed specifically to be a hallway and nothing more. At
the end of the hall, pale yellow light bled from a partially
cracked door.

He felt a little nervous. He had no idea what to expect.
He reached the door, put his hand on it, and took a deep
breath.

He pushed it open to reveal a withered, hunchbacked
crone with wildly frizzy hair standing in the middle of the
room. Her right hand, gnarled and heavy-looking, was
roughly ten times the size of her left. A small camera hung
suspended from the far right corner of the room. He

couldn't imagine this place being under surveillance and still running the way it did. Otherwise, the room was completely empty. Just gray walls and the gray tiled floor.

"Come to be processed, eh?" the crone asked.

"Yeah, I guess. I heard this was the place."

"It is. It is."

He continued to hover around the door, not wanting to venture further into this emptiness. Since the crone was the only other person in the room, he couldn't help but think she would be vital to the processing process.

"Come closer." She beckoned with her normal hand.

"I'm not sure how to do this."

"Just do what I say. Come closer now."

Cautiously, he crept toward her.

"Closer," she hissed.

He moved closer.

"*Closer.*"

Closer still.

Once he was within arm's length of her, she looked him up and down and, for a brief and horrifying moment, he thought he was going to have to have sex with this awful creature.

"There there," she said. "Now this won't hurt a bit."

She hauled back her gigantic right hand and took a massive roundhouse slap at his face. Her hand tore into his cheek, the force knocking him across the room.

He barked out in pain, collapsing onto his stomach and holding his left cheek. It was bleeding profusely. It felt like hamburger meat against his palm.

Now the crone scampered over to him and he braced himself, thinking she was going to kick him or something. But she didn't. She pulled out a slender rod about a foot in length from her skirt and ran it over his body. She turned to the camera in the corner and shouted, "He's clear!"

He curled into a fetal position.

"Can you tell me what's going on?"

"My job is only to process."

"To process me for what?"

"Deeper into the night. They always tell prisoners that before sending them in to me. I don't know why they wouldn't have told you."

"Deeper into the night. Why do I have to be processed into the night? That doesn't make any sense."

"It makes perfect sense. You belong to the night now. You're a night person. Morning is dead."

"Morning is dead?"

"You'll never see another one. It's just night for you now. Night. All the time. The night has levels. You go deeper and deeper. You can look for morning all you want. You can wait as long as you want. You can see it coming. You can taste it and feel it and sense it in your sinuses but it won't come."

The door creaked open and two officers came into the room. One of them was dressed, though shabbily, as a cop. The other wore baby blue footed sleeping pajamas. Positioning themselves on either side of him, they hoisted him to his feet.

"Where are you taking me?"

"To your cell, douchebag."

He thought about struggling but knew there wasn't any reason. He could only go back through the police station and there were too many cops out there, unless they had all passed out by now. They dragged him back down the hall. The one in uniform pulled a comically huge key ring from his belt and unlocked the door to the cell with the man in the towel outfit.

"Why can't I have the empty one?"

"Saving it. Now get in there and shut the hell up. Besides, it's not empty."

They tossed him roughly into the cell. He went sliding across the sickly wet floor. He curled his left arm around his head and bled onto it.

The intense man rocked back and forth on his bed, the only one in the cell, and said, "So, you into frottage?" His voice was high and nasally.

Alvin continued to lie there with his head on his arm, smelling the ammonia on the floor. He didn't know if it was from piss or cleaner. "I don't know what that is."

"It's like, uh, rubbing up against each other, you know? We don't have to penetrate or anything. We could leave our clothes on, even. Although it's better without."

"I don't think I'm into frottage."

"Damn," the man said before going back to rocking. "I'm Lars, by the way."

"I'm Alvin."

"It's nice to meet you, Alvin."

"Nice to meet you too, Lars." He figured he might as well be nice to him. After all, they were both in the same boat.

"I really wish you were into frottage."

"Me too."

"Really? I mean, we could always try it. If you didn't like it we could stop."

"I'm kind of tired right now. I might try to rest for a little bit."

"Oh. All right. Okay."

Alvin tried to forget everything that had happened to him. Lars went back to rocking. The springs on the bed squeaked as he did this. Alvin managed to either drift off or pass out.

When he came to, Lars was humping him. He had mounted his buttocks and was thrusting against him. Alvin could feel his stiff penis.

Alvin batted at him with his right hand and tried to stand up.

Lars hopped off and jumped back on the bed. "Sorry. I'm so sorry. I couldn't help it."

His words were lost in the dizzy swim of Alvin's head. He pulled himself up to his knees, his body threatening to collapse, his stomach threatening to heave. Lars came over to him, helping him up, apologizing continuously. "I really am sorry. I just can't help myself. Don't you see that? I've got a condition. I'll do anything to make it up to you. Anything. Just say it. You wanna hump me? Here, you can hump me until you can't hump no more."

Alvin reached out a hand and put it on Lars's shoulder. "Will you just please be quiet? That's all I want you to do right now. Just be quiet... Can I have the bed?"

"Oh, sure, sure. It's all yours."

Alvin sat down on the bed and Lars stood twittering before him.

"Can you stop staring at me?"

"Definitely. Not staring anymore." Lars crossed the cell to the bars and looked out over the police station.

Alvin followed his gaze and, for just a few seconds, it looked like an actual police station. He smelled coffee in the air and saw real cops sitting around desks, typing things into computers, eating morning donuts. He saw what had to be secretaries and police dispatchers. Then it was gone. Back to the hobo cops. Most of them were sprawled out on the floor in various states of undress. The air was ripe with vice. One cop vomited into a trash can. Another cop wore a bib and sat devouring something that looked like a roasted dog.

Alvin delicately touched his cheek and tried to think of a way out.

A Hospital at Night
Part Five

Still sitting in the chair, April leaned her head forward until her face rested in the bleachy smell of the bed. She closed her eyes. She was exhausted. It overwhelmed her all at once. The sounds she had picked out and individualized all swirled together and pulled into some kind of vacuum.

She dreamed about floating in space. It was black and numb. She couldn't see the earth anywhere.

When she awoke, the beeping from Alvin's monitor had stopped.

Five

Alvin continued to sit on the bed and hold his head in his hands, his cheek throbbing sickly. Lars humped the bars of the cell and made moaning sounds he was barely able to keep in check. A number of the officers were coming to. They moved about the station, lighting cigarettes, making coffee, and exchanging stories of the previous night's exploits. From what Alvin was able to gather, they sounded more like a gang, moving through the streets at night, breaking into people's homes, abducting and raping women and men, jumping people, killing animals and rades. Through the doors at the front of the station, Alvin could see that it was still dark outside, even though he thought it looked like the sky was lightening only moments before. Maybe he had dozed off without realizing it. Maybe he had dozed off for a really long time.

Fuckpants stood at Bitchhole's desk, a cigarette dangling from the corner of his mouth. He held up Bitchhole's right arm and watched it limply drop back down onto the desk. He did it several more times. His eyes looked blank. Then he felt around Bitchhole's neck.

"I think we got an OD," he said calmly and to no one in particular. Ash dropped from the end of his cigarette and scattered on the desk with a slow, dreamlike motion.

A fat cop wearing black leather pants said, "I'll drag him down to the incinerator."

"Sounds like a good idea," Fuckpants said. He pulled Bitchhole's chair away from the desk and rolled him onto the floor. Then he sat down in the chair and put his feet up on the desk. He threw his head back and exhaled a languid cloud of smoke toward the ceiling. Alvin thought he saw an image in the smoke and squinted hard to make it out but by the time he thought he almost had it the smoke had dissipated.

Alvin felt someone poking him on the back.

He turned his head. It was the homeless-looking man. The man held his hand through the bars. Alvin shook it. It was rough and grimy.

"You're Alvin?"

"Yeah."

"I'm Benjamin Teats."

"Teats?"

"Yes."

"It's nice to meet you." Alvin could smell Benjamin from where he sat on the bed. Urine, grime, and feces.

"I heard your story. Out there. About your wife?"

"Yes."

"That's a shame. I'm guessing you'd like to get out of here."

"More than anything, at this point."

"I might be able to help you with that."

Maybe it was just Benjamin's appearance, but Alvin immediately assumed he was crazy. Still, there was a faint flicker of hope. "If you know how to get out then why are you still here?"

"I have no reason to get out. I have nothing to go back home for. My morning, my days, before I came here, were filled with nothing. Just sitting around the house and watching television. Here, at least, there are a lot more entertaining things than television. And, occasionally, if they're wasted enough, they'll toss a girl my way."

"Ah," Alvin said. "So it's sex? I've always assumed most things come down to either money or sex."

Benjamin paused to think about that. "You might be right. But what about love?"

"Well, I think you usually want to have sex with someone before you realize you love them and, if you have children, you probably love them, but they are almost always the product of sex. But I think we got sidetracked. You were going to tell me how to get out of here."

"Yes. I was. So why do you want out? Is it money or sex?"

"Love."

"I see."

They both released a resigned sigh.

"You noticed it, didn't you?" Benjamin asked.

"Noticed what?"

"The morning. You saw it."

Alvin thought about the couple of seconds when his surroundings resembled a functional police station.

"I don't know what I saw."

"Think of being wrapped in a cocoon of misery. The night. For just a moment, there is a break in that cocoon. It has to have a momentary break or else it just is. If the night people never experienced a shred of the morning, night would lose its meaning. And there must be a point to the endless night, although I haven't found it yet."

"Is it possible to escape back into the day? To outlast the night?"

Benjamin laughed softly and placed a hand on Alvin's shoulder. "I'm afraid not. There may be a way to do that but, if there is, I haven't heard about it yet. When the morning occurs, there is merely a momentary break in this reality. A flash of chaos. Maybe it isn't even real. Maybe it's just a collective hallucination. Mass hysteria."

"Is that when I should try to get out? Will I have to wait until tomorrow?"

"There is no tomorrow here. Like I said, it's just something that happens. It doesn't have any specific time. The time here is measured by when those yokels pass out." He motioned to the cops lackadaisically milling around the station. "Out there, maybe it's measured by something else. Maybe one day ends and the next begins when your car runs out of gas. Or when you get snagged by a rade. Or maybe just when you pass out from confusion and exhaustion. Believe me, the day you left behind is not the night you have entered."

"I'm not sure what I left behind. I have trouble remembering what the daytime was like. So how do I get out?"

"Oh, it's really pretty simple, if you're serious about it."

"I am. I can't stay here."

"You just have to start banging your head against the bars. I've seen it work. Although it's been quite some time ago. Regardless, I haven't seen it used so many times that the cops have caught on to it. Maybe three times at the most."

"That's all I have to do?"

"Well, you have to really mean it. You really have to ram your head into those things. But not so much that you knock yourself unconscious. What you do is you *pretend* to knock yourself unconscious. Now, the worst-case scenario is that they just leave you to lie on the floor. But, I have my suspicions about this place. I think they use the prisoners for something. I think they need us alive. I think we're like societal abortions…"

"Societal abortions?"

Teats waved a dismissive hand. "You don't want to hear about that."

"So I really have to lay into it, huh?"

"Yes, and if you're lucky, they'll have to open the door to check on you. They're usually pretty stoned and out of it, especially the longer they're on duty. There might be two or three of them to come in and check on you. If they were smart or sober or aware, at least one of them would probably have his gun drawn, but I wouldn't count on that happening. We could work something out. I could cough really loud if one of them has his gun drawn. You won't know, see, because you'll be pretending to be out cold."

Alvin thought about it. It sounded painful. But he was already in a lot of pain. His cheek still throbbed and burned. It sounded risky. It almost sounded like the stupidest idea in the world but he couldn't really think of anything better. Then he thought of something else.

"Don't they let us out periodically to shower or go to a lunchroom or an exercise yard or something?"

"The only time I've ever seen people leave the cells was to be processed or disappear completely."

"What do you mean by disappear completely? When they get released?"

"If they're getting released, they're not leaving by the front door. It's all a bit peculiar."

"How do I know one of them won't shoot me in the back?"

"Their aim isn't that great even when they are straight. If I see one of them go for his gun, I could try to create a distraction. It'll only take you a couple seconds to get to the front door. They'll probably be too lazy to follow you. It's not like they're real cops or anything."

Alvin thought he would probably go for it. He supposed, at this point, there really wasn't any guessing the outcome.

"I have something for you. For when you get out."

Benjamin's optimism made Alvin feel good. He handed Alvin a piece of paper folded in half. Alvin started to open it and Benjamin stopped him by placing a hand over his. "Wait until you get out to open it. Keep it in your pocket until then. It's the address of a safe house. A buddy of mine. He'll help you."

Alvin folded the paper further and stuck it into his pocket. "Thanks."

Alvin lay back on the bed and stared up at the dirty ceiling. After a while, an officer came to the door of the cell. He had a huge handlebar mustache and wore a sparkling cape with his uniform. The name above his pocket read: ASSCLOWN and was written in marker on a piece of masking tape.

"Hey, Humper," the cop said.

"Yeah?" Lars asked.

"The Processor wants to see you."

"But I've already been processed."

The cop twisted the tips of his mustache and said, "I didn't say she wants to process you. I said she wants to see you."

"Well, okay," Lars said. He slumped his shoulders in fear and dejection.

The cop slid the cell door open and took Lars by the arm. He banged the cell door shut and led Lars down the hall. A few minutes later, Alvin heard terrible screams. He would never see Lars again. He didn't know if he was sad about that. He wondered why he didn't go for his escape when the cell door was open. That seemed liked it would be easier than ramming his head into the bars. But he had already planned to ram his head into the bars. He wasn't expecting to escape when the doors were open to fetch Lars. His body, his muscles weren't ready for that. He would have to be fast. He would have to charge for the doors and pray a bullet didn't come ripping through his body.

Lars's screams continued for quite some time. Alvin lay back on his tiny bed, separated from Benjamin and his horrible stink only by the bars between them, trying to muster up the courage to ram his head into the bars and escape.

"Can I call you 'Ben'?" Alvin asked.

"You can call me anything. Names aren't really important."

"Okay. Good. How long has it been since you've bathed or showered?"

"A very long time."

"What do you think they're doing to Lars?"

"Something painful."

"Obviously. He's not coming back, is he?"

"No. I try not to think about what they do to the people who leave. Rather, I like to think they just vanish. I like to think they go to see the Processor and then just disintegrate into millions of pieces, float away like water vapor, like mist. But I know that isn't true. Humans are a commodity. Life is a commodity. They need it for something. Something secret."

"Who's they?"

"Probably has something to do with the Point. Either the Point gets you or the rades get you."

"Is there any purpose behind it? Why would they need humans? For like… sacrifice or something."

"I'm not really sure. I have a number of ideas. *Had* a number of ideas. Like I said, I don't really like to think about it. But I've been out there. I know about the abortion clinic, too."

"The abortion clinic?"

"That, I *refuse* to talk about."

"So it could happen to me or you? We could be called back to the Processor's?"

"Any moment. Although they usually space them apart. And I think they've stopped noticing me."

Finally, Lars's screams stopped. The station was mostly empty now. Officer Assclown sat at the desk toward the front of the office.

"Time is weird here," Alvin said. Looking out at the station was like watching, by turns, elapsed time and slow motion. Now the station appeared nearly full again.

"Yes, it most definitely is."

"So what do you do all day?"

"Night, you mean?"

"Whatever."

"Mostly just lie here. Sometimes I beat off."

"Ah, that can't help the smell very much."

"No. It makes me sweat and then I usually just come in my pants or all over the bed. So there's that, also."

"No sense in really putting up a front, huh?"

"Not really. Everyone is here for some reason or the other. We are 'nonproductive' members of society."

"I think Fuckpants mentioned something about that."

"They usually don't go into too much detail."

"You know, I used to work at the Point."

"Everybody has, at some time or the other. For them or one of their affiliates."

"Did you?"

"No."

"Where did you work?"

"I had my own business. I was a mortician. Everyone who died was either a worker at the Point, a former worker at the Point, or a spouse or child of someone who worked at the Point so I guess you could still stay I worked for the Point."

"I understand that I may have ceased being a productive member of society when I lost my job, but how does a mortician become nonproductive?"

"People stopped dying."

"I thought you might say something like that."

"I think maybe they came here. To the night. Or maybe, because life is such a commodity, somebody decided not to wait around until people died."

"I don't see how they could get away with something like that."

"When you have your tentacles into everything, you can get away with anything."

Alvin liked that description. Or, he didn't like it. It horrified him. He liked it because it horrified him. Ben had described it just right. The Point ceased being a plant where people went to work and became some Lovecraftian creature, stretched out into every aspect of the city, into every home, squeezing the souls and pockets and brains and balls of every resident.

"I think they're harvesting tissue. But then there's the incinerator… I think that's what they do with the dead… if they don't get to them in time…"

A tremble ran through Ben. He swiped his hands out in front of himself like he was batting a spider web.

"That's okay," Alvin said. "Don't think about it. I'm not sure I want to know anyway. I just want to get back home. They've rigged it up."

"Rigged it up?"

"For detonation."

"Oh God… It's true then. I'd heard about that." Another tremor ran through Ben, this one so fierce his bed shook and squeaked. He put his hand over his eyes and opened his mouth. A low, almost subsonic, squeal came out.

"Forget I said it." Alvin tapped a knuckle on the bar. "Don't worry about it."

Ben stopped squealing, put his arms back to his sides, and they lay there in silence for a bit. Alvin tried to think of questions to ask Ben. But he didn't want to ask him anything having to do with the Point or death or the night or, apparently, the detonations. Ben had been here a long time. He might know the answers. In fact, he had led Alvin to believe that he had a number of theories. Alvin consoled himself by thinking he probably didn't want to know the answers or theories anyway. There didn't seem to be a lot of promise contained in this grim night world.

"I think you should come with me," Alvin said.

"Huh?"

"When I try to make my break... I think you should

come with me."

"I couldn't possibly do that."

"Sure you can. You're just lonely. You need to get out of here."

"The sex is worth staying in for."

"When you were a mortician, did you ever have sex with a corpse?"

"All the time."

"That's what I thought."

"They're dead, right? What does it matter?"

Alvin had his own opinions about that but didn't think Ben would really want to hear them. Especially not if he was trying to cajole him into coming along with him.

"Besides," Ben said, "there's nothing for me out there."

"But don't you have a home? Isn't there anything for you there?"

"I lost everything. I had a wife. A daughter and a son. A *very* nice house. And then… nothing."

"But you could start all over again. You're not that old. Think about it. You could buy your own prostitutes. You could have some control over your life. Is your house still standing? Maybe you could make amends with your wife. Surely your children would like to see you."

"This is easier."

"Maddening."

Ben rolled over onto his side, facing away from Alvin, and farted, washing Alvin in the stink of death. Alvin coughed. He felt like he couldn't breathe. He stood up and moved closer to the bars. He had that sensation of worlds overlapping again. Could an entire day have passed already? No, that was impossible. Besides, Ben said it didn't have anything to do with real time anyway.

There were only three cops in the station. Only Officer Assclown appeared to be conscious. The place smelled of liquor, smoke, and puke. Alvin looked at Ben lying there on his bed and thought about himself, growing old in that cell. Or worse, ending up like Lars.

"I'm going to do it now," Alvin said.

Ben rolled over onto his back and nodded.

Alvin grabbed the bars and rammed his head into them.

Assclown looked toward him and shook his head. Alvin rammed his head again and again. He felt blood running down into his eyes. His skull throbbed. He rammed his head until he was just on the brink of consciousness and then slipped down onto the floor. He heard footsteps approach the cell, keys jangling and then hesitating.

"You'd better check him out," Ben said. "I think he's hurt pretty bad."

"Shut the fuck up, Stink."

Lying on the disgusting floor of the cell, his cheek and forehead raw meat, in a growing pool of his own blood, Alvin felt a moment of joy as he heard the keys enter the cell door. As the door slid open he strained to hear if Ben coughed or not. Not hearing anything, Alvin leapt up and took off running for the doors. He felt something hit him in the back, probably the keys, and then he was outside, running for one of the cars parked on the curb.

He tripped over something and went sprawling.

He glanced quickly over his shoulder as he stood back up and saw a cop sprawled face down in a puddle of vomit, an empty bottle of tequila just out of arm's reach.

Assclown stood just outside the doors of the station, struggling to unholster his weapon, shouting, "Jailbreak! Jailbreak!"

Morning is Dead

Alvin charged a few more strides. He quickly surveyed the line of recklessly parked cars in front of the station and leapt into the first one he came to, hoping for the best.

He heard shots. They didn't even hit the car.

He checked the steering column. Keys dangled from it. A bottle opener emblazoned with a beer logo hung down from the key chain. Alvin looked back at the station to see another officer putting his arm around Assclown. It looked like he was trying to talk him into going back into the station and just forgetting about everything. Alvin twisted the key in the ignition and, realizing it was already running, pounded the accelerator and roared out into the night.

A Hospital at Night
Part Six

April looked at the monitor. It was odd that the beeping had stopped. She had never heard this happen. Usually it went from beeping to a flatline. This time there was no sound. She didn't think that could be good. She stood up from the chair and looked at the monitor. There wasn't a spiky line. There wasn't a flat line. There wasn't any line. The box with the "call nurse" button on it dangled off the bed. She could press the button. She was a nurse but she didn't know what to do. Would Mirabel know what to do? Would the doctor on duty know what to do? Did she want Alvin to be revived if his heart had stopped beating?

April's heart pounded. She reached down to manually take his pulse at the wrist but it was covered in bandages. Everything was covered in bandages except for his closed eyes. She thought about pressing the side of his neck, where the pulse was usually strong.

She didn't.

She looked down at him. Looking at him hurt something inside of her. He could be anyone. He was a mummy with tubes, like some monster from an old sci-fi movie.

She imagined him wandering through the hospital, stiff like a mummy, wrapped in all that gauze, tubes snaking out from him like tentacles, waiting to latch on to someone else and suck the life from them.

She shuddered.

The monitor started up again.

It startled her and she jumped and then she cried out and sat down and put her hands over her mouth to stifle a laugh.

Mirabel's hand was on her shoulder. "Are you okay?"

"Yeah... I'm... No, I'm not okay. I don't think so, Mir." She took a deep shaky breath. "The monitor stopped. It was the strangest thing."

"Did he go flat?"

"No. It just stopped. There wasn't anything there at all." April stood up. "Would you have a cigarette?"

"In my purse. It's at the station. You know which one it is?"

April nodded. "I just need to step out for a minute."

"I'll stay here. I'll watch him."

April left the hospital room.

Six

He checked the rearview mirror to make sure none of the cops decided to pursue him. There wasn't anything there. He turned around just in time to slam on the brakes.

A man shuffled across the street. He looked old and homeless and didn't move very quickly. A rade stalked along behind him. Alvin thought about running over it but he seemed frozen, unable to do anything. He sat in the idling car. The rade fell upon the man. The man screamed and slapped his thin arms out against the rade. Alvin was suddenly conscious of the blood running down his face, masking it. The rade's victim looked right at the police car, into the police car, into Alvin. The man would never be able to identify Alvin. Was that why he just sat here and watched? He wanted to leave the scene. He wanted to drive past it and clip the rade, make him stop. The rade pinned the man's arms on the ground over his head. The man gradually stopped struggling. The rade seemed to grow even brighter. It looked like the rade was naked but it didn't have any sex to it. He remembered what Fuckpants had said about their needlelike fingertips. But Fuckpants had been mostly full of shit. Didn't Ben mention the rades, too? Alvin was sure he did. He said they were some kind of refuse from the Point. Or had Fuckpants said that?

Soon, the rade's victim stopped struggling altogether.

The rade stood up with dripping fingertips and wandered off into the night as if he was too full to move quickly.

Alvin finally pulled the car forward. He looked at the man on the ground. Pinpricks of green glowed where the rade's needles had penetrated him. As Alvin watched, the green began to spread. The man's clothes were sizzling, smoke or steam rising up from the body. Alvin gunned the car. He couldn't think of anything worse than watching this man who had been alive only moments before become something else, something that wasn't even human.

The fat officer still slept in the back seat. Alvin must have appropriated Fuckpants's car, if the officers were even assigned cars. They probably just took what they wanted. The fat man didn't stir as Alvin tore through downtown, taking turns on two wheels and not bothering to stop for lights or stop signs. He had to get home. He had to get home and find a way to get in the house. He didn't know who had moved in in his place but he knew it couldn't be good. It either meant April was cheating on him or she was in serious danger. She could even be dead by this point. He didn't really know how long he was in the prison. In retrospect, it seemed like only a few hours, but it could have been days. The more he thought about it the longer it seemed.

Looking around at all the darkened houses of the sleeping suburbs, he saw more rades than he thought he would. They would have been impossible to spot had it not been for their glowing skin. Most of them seemed to be deep in the alleyways. He wondered what it was they really did. If they mostly tried to hide out because they were such abominations, they weren't doing a very good job of it. And the rade he had seen feasting on that man seemed like such an easy target. Only Alvin didn't do anything about it. Maybe they had some strange kind of hypnotic power. Maybe that was why their skin glowed. To soothe the eyes and then reach in and lull some part of the soul.

Alvin pulled the car up to the curb in front of his house. In keeping with police protocol, he didn't bother shutting it off or even closing the door. The men were still up on the roof working. Wires covered nearly the entire house. It was starting to look like the inside of some old electronic device. A stereo, maybe.

"Hey!" he called up to them.

No one answered him.

"This is my house! Can you tell me what you're doing up there? Nobody asked you to do this."

A man walked to the end of the roof and stared down at him through his ominous gas mask. He reached into his black coveralls and pulled out a rolled up piece of paper. He let it drop off the roof and it landed in front of Alvin's feet. He picked it up and unrolled it. The only word he could identify was "Contract". The rest of it seemed to be in some kind of gibberish. It seemed like it would make sense if he thought really hard about it but he seemed incapable of thinking hard about anything. He didn't want to appear stupid so he just rolled the piece of paper back up and then dropped it where it had landed before.

He walked up to the front door and began pounding on it.

There was no answer for a long time.

He continued to pound.

Morning is Dead

Someone had to be in there. What if that strange man *had* done something to April? What if she *was* dead?

He knocked harder, the door shaking in its frame.

Then it opened.

That weird man who looked kind of like him stood in the doorway. Alvin tried to push his way through. The man put his hands on Alvin's chest and pushed him back out onto the front porch.

"This is *my* house," Alvin said.

"No," the man said. He was calm. His voice was empty of any emotion and, staring at him, his eyes were just as void. "This is not your house."

"Who are *you*? What the fuck do you want with my house? With my *wife*?"

The man looked at him. He straightened the front of his expensive suit. "I am you," he said. "My name is Alvin Blue. This is my house. April Blue is my wife. I... mate with her."

"No!" Alvin said. "You're not me. You do *not* mate with my wife!"

"Goodbye." The man tried to shut the door but Alvin managed to stop it.

The man continued forcing the door closed. He was very strong. Alvin continued to push against it. Then the man let go of the door and Alvin went flying into him. He put his arms around Alvin and dragged him out to the porch.

"HELP!" Alvin shouted. There had to be someone to hear him. Everyone couldn't sleep that soundly. Everyone couldn't be asleep at the same time. Why didn't one of the workers on the roof come down to help him? At least to break them up.

The man was larger than Alvin and he felt more solid.

He carried Alvin down the porch stairs and pushed him onto the front lawn. Alvin went sprawling onto his back.

"Stay away," the man said.

Alvin kicked at him. The man casually walked over, raised his foot, and brought it down on Alvin's stomach. The pain was sharp and spread through his entire torso.

"Next time I will stomp the throat of you."

Who the fuck *was* this? Alvin thought.

"I'm coming back," Alvin said.

"Unlikely," the man said, already back on the porch.

"I'll find out what the hell's going on and I'll stop you."

The man made something like a laugh. Then he looked at Alvin and drew his finger across his throat like he had when Alvin first found himself locked out. He walked inside and shut the door. Alvin heard the locks click shut.

He stood up as straight as possible. His stomach hurt incredibly and he had to double over. He wondered if something had ruptured. He had no idea what to do now. He guessed he could try and find some store that would have weaponry. Then he could come back armed. If he could get the man to come to the door again, he would not hesitate to hurt him. If the police wouldn't help him then he would have to help himself. He tried to straighten himself and began walking back to the car. He stopped once he rounded the corner of the house. The car was covered in rades.

Sensing him, they turned en masse and began walking toward him. He took off in the opposite direction, east down Thistle, toward the alley. He heard them behind him. He wondered what it would feel like when they finally got their needles into his neck, pumping him full of radiation while drawing his life out. He rounded the corner into the alley and tried the first garage door he came to. Locked. He ran further down and tried another one. Locked. Damn.

The rades turned into the alleyway. There weren't any streetlights back here and that was to Alvin's advantage. He could see the rades much better than they could see him. He charged through the nearest backyard, up toward the house. They had a wooden back porch just like his. He quickly checked the bottom of it to make sure it also contained puny lattice and not a solid foundation like brick or concrete. Moving slower now, he pulled back the lattice and slid under the porch. It was gross. It was damp. It smelled like cat piss and shit. God only knew what else was under there. But if it kept the rades from finding him, that was all he could hope for. He watched as their horde marched down the alley.

But one stayed behind. He saw its head turn toward him. It began walking through the yard. As it drew closer, Alvin's heart once again sped up. He had backed himself into a corner. He seriously doubted he would be able to fight his way out of it. The thing looked like the drawings he had seen of aliens except it didn't seem to have any mouth whatsoever and its nails were so razor sharp and needlelike that he didn't even notice them until it was standing less than two feet away. It leaned down and Alvin knew he was done for.

And then it just kept leaning until it came down on the grass head first.

This was his chance to make a break for it. He bolted out from under the porch and stopped when he heard a voice say, "It's okay, friend. It can't hurt you now."

It was a voice he kind of recognized. When he turned around, the first thing he noticed was an arrow sticking out the back of the rade's head. To the right stood the archer.

"This one's dead," the archer said. "But I don't think we should linger. The others will be coming back soon enough."

"What are we going to do about...?"

"Leave it. Someone'll come along and pick it up."

The archer tugged his arrow from the back of the rade's skull and gave it a wipedown in the grass.

"Thanks," Alvin said. "I thought I was dead there for a second."

"You would have been. Well, not dead, but one of them."

They walked side by side through the yard and back out into the alley where they turned left, away from the horde of rades.

A Hospital at Night
Part Seven

April took only one cigarette from Mirabel's purse. One cigarette, a lighter, and her cardigan that was slung over the back of a chair. If she took more than one cigarette, she knew she would have stood outside until they were all gone. She didn't want to go back into Alvin's room.

She draped the sweater over her shoulders. It smelled clean, like a dryer sheet. It made her realize how dirty she felt. She smelled like smoke. Her lungs still burned but she wanted the cigarette anyway. She wanted to draw even more smoke into her lungs. She wanted to show it she had power over it. Smoke was something wild and uncontrollable. Smoking was one way to harness it.

As she walked toward the elevator, the rest of the hospital seemed too bright. At this hour, it was calm. Like most nights. Dayton was a city of much minutiae and false alarms. The weekends were usually more eventful. The elevator doors opened with only a second's hesitation and she stepped into it, thankful to be alone.

On the way down, she thought about the time Brett had beaten Alvin up. He hadn't really beaten him up. In truth,

April had never even asked him about it. She didn't want to know. She loved Alvin but he had embarrassed her. She had just wanted him to go away. She had heard him try to get in one night, pounding on the door. Brett said he would go downstairs and see who it was, what they wanted, even though he and April both knew who it was. She had stayed in bed, the phone within arm's reach, ready to call the police if anything got of control. Brett was back upstairs within two minutes.

"Did you take care of it?" April had asked.

"It was nothing," Brett had said.

And they had left it at that.

The elevator stopped and April strolled out through the lobby. The receptionist on duty, a large black woman whose name April couldn't remember, nodded at her. April nodded back. With her good arm, she pulled the cardigan tighter around her and stepped out into the chilly night. She walked fifty feet from the front door, to the smoking area, and sat down on the wooden slatted bench. She crossed her legs and drew into herself as much as she could, making herself as small as possible or trying to capture the warmth. She lit the cigarette and looked up at the sky. It looked weird. It was cloudy but it must have been close to a full moon because the clouds glowed an eerie gray white. It almost didn't seem as late as it was. The city was quieter now but there was still the sound of trains and the unclosing factories.

April continued to smoke and stare out at the night. It reached in and around her, stroking her with cold fingers. She felt more alone than she ever had. Maybe that was what drew Alvin into the night. She didn't know if it was something mental, like some switch inside of him that had simply flipped, or if the drugs had made him that way. She wondered what had started him on drugs anyway. Maybe it was something he had done before he met her and then stopped because she was something new only to start up again when he got bored. It was shortly after his friend, John Strange, had moved back into the area. Maybe that was what they did, although Alvin never really mentioned hanging around with him. John Strange and Brian Tippin. April hadn't thought about those names in a long time. Brian Tippin had always lived in the area but he and Alvin had never really hung out much because Brian was married and had a couple of kids. But then he had gotten a divorce and started calling a little more often. He was probably lonely. April thought she knew how he felt.

There was a secret world going on around her, April thought. That was a funny thought to have. But it was true. There were people just like Alvin, wandering around downtown, driving through the suburbs, planning ludicrous things. Lost people. Directionless people. Whores working the streets for drug money or strippers in some smelly club working for drug money or to put food on the table for their kids or to put themselves through college. Junkies and alcoholics hanging around outside bars, begging for just enough money to feed their addiction. And then there were the people working in the factories, gray faced and glassy eyed, standing at some machine that dictated their pace. Dictated eight or ten or sometimes twelve or fourteen hours of their day. And some of those people were crazier than the people wandering the streets. And some of the people wandering the streets weren't crazy at all. They just didn't want any part of normal life. They would rather have this life of pain and despair because that meant they were doing something, it sparked some sense of adventure in them.

April put her cigarette out in the sand of the stone ash-tray beside the bench and thought about standing up and drifting off into the night. She could just disappear. She wouldn't have to find out what happened to Alvin. She wouldn't have to mourn him if he died and she wouldn't have to care for him if he lived.

She felt cold, inside and out, and she hated to think she would resent taking care of him. But then she thought about Brett and how he was gone and what that had taken from her and she thought about how perfect, for a while, every-thing had been between she and Alvin, and how that was gone too.

The early October air sliced against her ear. It wanted her. The night wanted her. In a way, she longed for it too.

Seven

Walking along beside the archer, Alvin looked back over his shoulder. "Thanks for your help and everything, but I really need to get back to my house. Someone is in there with my wife. And they're putting wires up everywhere. All over the house. Covering it in wires. The cops told me that meant they were going to blow it up."

"Relax, friend. There's no point in going back now."

The archer continued walking down the dark alleyway. Alvin kept up with him. Maybe he could tell him something that made sense.

"Why not? Why is there no point in going back?"

"Have you been to the station? Have you been processed?"

"Yeah, but I don't see what that has to do with anything."

"Unfortunately, that has everything to do with everything."

"Why? Please say you can tell me why. No one's been able to tell me anything."

"Because you're part of the night now. You're a night person."

"But what does that mean?"

"It's pretty simple really. There's the day and there's the night."

"But there's always been day and night. When I was, I guess, part of the day, it still became night. Don't tell me there's someplace where it's day all the time?"

"No, there isn't. You're right. When you were part of the day, it did become night. But that was natural night. That was the natural world. This is not the natural world. That's the best way to think of it—as two separate worlds."

"Two separate worlds."

The archer's breath was steady. The gravel of the alley crunched beneath their feet. Alvin could feel himself getting further away from the house, further from April, further from any type of logic at all.

"Yes, two separate worlds."

"But how is that possible?"

"It's kind of a mystery, I guess. But it happens. One minute, you're part of that world and the next minute you're part of this world."

"So am I dead?"

"Not technically."

Alvin grabbed the sides of his head in frustration. His hair was crusted with dried blood. He was suddenly aware of the smell of the blood, sick and meaty.

"So, what? What am I?"

"I take it you worked for the Point?"

"Yeah, but so what? Everybody works for the Point or something that serves the Point in some way or the other."

"Not everyone."

"You never worked for the Point? What did you do before you became a night person?"

"Of course I worked for the Point. But I've always been a night person. The Point steals something from you. It makes you something you weren't before."

"Are you talking about a soul?"

"No. Not necessarily. Just some essential part of what it feels like to be alive. What makes being alive something special. Think about before you started working at the Point: what made life good then? What did you enjoy doing?"

"Lots of things: falling in love with April, listening to music, watching movies. I liked doing things outside. Walking around downtown and drinking coffee on a spring day..."

"And once you started working for the Point?"

"Well, things were pretty good. We both had good jobs. We bought a house in this neighborhood... it's not too bad." Alvin thought as he walked beside the archer. Surely they had done more things. Surely there was something he could remember. "And then..."

"And then?"

"I don't know."

"And then you started working more so you could keep up with those house payments and you started seeing less and less of your wife and maybe you thought about having kids but you knew you would both have to work even harder to support the kid so what was the point in bringing a kid into the world if you couldn't even enjoy it? And after you got home from work you were so exhausted and lifeless that you just sat around watching television and doing the essential things like eating and shitting and showering that you didn't really have time for anything else. And even on the weekends you were so full of dread and loathing about going back to work on Monday that you couldn't possibly enjoy them fully. Maybe you started going out by yourself. Maybe you started hanging around with people you shouldn't have been hanging around with, doing some things you weren't supposed to be doing. But, goddammit, you were just trying to have a little *fun*. You were just trying to relax and unwind."

Alvin hung his head. It pained him to admit these things. "Yeah, actually, that sounds about right."

"It's not your fault," the archer said. "It happens to just about everyone."

"But what kind of punishment is *this*? Being banished into some world where the sun never shines. Where I'll never see my wife again. *Am* I being punished for something?"

"I couldn't possibly answer that. Besides, you'll probably see your wife eventually. Almost everyone gets worn down at some time or the other. The city's designed that way."

They reached an intersection with another alley. A short, rumpled-looking man stared at a garage. Alvin didn't even notice him until they were right up on him. A dead, mangled, and emaciated dog lay at his feet. The man had gore around his mouth and down the front of his shirt. Alvin was pretty sure he had been eating the dog.

"Maria!" the man shouted at the garage.

The archer stopped and Alvin stopped along with him.

"MARIA!!!" the man shouted again. Then, noticing them, the man whipped his head around, looked at Alvin, and said, "You seen Maria? I bet you have, ain't ya, Mr. Bloodyface?" He drew closer to Alvin until he could smell some kind of boozy, decaying reek coming from him and the scent of the dead dog was now obvious.

"No." Alvin held out his hand to ward the man off. "I don't even know who Maria is."

"Don't lie to me. I'll reach down your fuckin' throat and pull Maria out. Yeah, I'll punch a hole in that blood mask. You think it's Halloween? You think it's trick-or-treat yet? No. It ain't. You don't even got a fuckin' bag. No sack for treats, Mr. Bloodyface."

The archer had tugged an arrow from his quiver and Alvin thought he was going to stab the man but, instead, he swatted him on the upper arm with the arrow. "You need to calm down, Clarence. Go back inside and be quiet. Maria will be around shortly."

Clarence looked at the archer. He pointed to the house on the other side of the garage and whispered, "There are people in there. Sleeping people."

Alvin's heart thumped. Yes, this man knew about all the sleepers too.

"You're just imagining them, Clarence. There's no one in there. You live alone, remember?"

"Maybe Maria'll be in there?" he asked hopefully.

"You'll have to go in and check, Clarence."

"Okay." Now he sounded kind of excited as he turned and walked toward the house.

The archer and Alvin continued down the alley.

"Where are we going?" Alvin asked.

"My place."

After the exchange with the Maria-shouter, Alvin was under the assumption the night people shared houses with the sleeping daytime people. If he was able to get back into his house, he wondered if he would find April asleep. No, that was ridiculous. He'd just seen her a couple of days ago. The same night that strange man had appeared. And he had just fought with that strange man only moments ago. So they weren't asleep. Unless April was dead or in trouble. Which Alvin still felt was a distinct possibility.

Alvin stopped. "I really need to go back to my house."

"I told you. It's useless."

"I have to try."

"You can spend the rest of your life trying. It won't do any good. Look, I might be able to use your help. You help me and I'll help you. Okay?"

"Help you with what?"

"I'll tell you. But I have something for you to see first."

"Are there any sleepers at your place?"

"No. It's just me. Why?"

"I'm just curious about them."

"Why?"

"I'm not sure. Have you ever tried waking one of them up?"

"Nope. I figure they're asleep for a reason. Here we go." The archer stopped at a long, low structure.

"This is your house?"

"This is part of it. Most of the house is underground. This is my warehouse. I call it the Shucking Room."

"The Shucking Room?" Alvin imagined corn.

"You'll see."

The archer pulled a set of keys from his pocket and unlocked the barn-style door, sliding it back. He stepped into the structure and flipped a switch. Harsh fluorescent lights blared down from the ceiling. The light stinging his eyes, Alvin tried to make out what it was he was looking at.

"Are those..."

"Rades. Yeah."

There had to be ten of them. They weren't moving. They were lined up in two rows, dangling from large hooks. There was another row of empty hooks hanging from the ceiling, coated in dull green.

"What do you do with them?"

"You'll see."

"Do you mind if I wash up?"

"Go ahead."

The archer motioned to an industrial sink in the back corner.

The archer slid the door closed and snapped a padlock shut around a short chain. The floor of the Shucking Room was smooth concrete. The air held an ozone tang like before a storm.

Alvin walked back to the sink. He turned the faucet on warm and splashed it over his face, trying to clean out his cheek and forehead wounds as best as possible. Once the water dripping from his face was clear, he switched it to cold and splashed some of that on his face to try and revive him. He pulled his t-shirt up and wiped his face with it. He began walking back toward the archer.

The archer grabbed something like a metal cane, wrapped it around the top of one of the hooks, and pulled it toward a stainless steel slab. He donned a pair of thick rubber gloves that came up to his elbows and, grabbing the rade beneath the arms, lifted it off the hook. It made a sick meaty sound. He sat it on the slab. Then he took several steps, grabbed a large metal drum on wheels, and dragged it beside the table.

"Can you bring that over here?" he nodded toward a metal canister, about the size of a soda can. Alvin grabbed it and brought it over.

He sat the can-thing down beside the larger barrel. Then he remembered the piece of paper Ben had given him. He reached into his pocket and pulled it out. It was an address. "Hm."

"What's that?"

"Do you know where this might be?" Alvin handed the paper to the archer.

"It's not very far away."

"I've never even heard of the street name."

"Help me out here and I'll take you there. Who gave this to you?"

"Some guy I met at the station."

"What was the guy's name?"

Alvin chuckled. "Benjamin Teats."

"Why are you laughing?"

"Teats?" He thought about explaining it and realized the archer probably still wouldn't think it was funny.

"What's your name, by the way?" The archer pulled back his hood. Long, reddish hair dropped to his shoulders. With his beard, he looked like some kind of hill dweller.

"I'm Alvin Blue."

"I'm Jeffrey Suckle. But most everyone calls me Archer."

"You don't see many people with bows and arrows."

"I guess not."

He pulled what looked like a pair of gardening shears from the large drum.

"Now," he said, "the first thing you want to do is remove the fingers so you don't get poked. They can hurt you even when dead."

With the rade's hand resting on the table, Archer began clipping off the ends of the fingers.

69

"What exactly are you doing with them?"

"Removing their skin."

"Why?"

"Well, some of it I sell back to the Point. Isn't that funny? They create these things by some sort of accident and then have to pay me for their skin. But they only want so much. Actually, they only want to pay me so much. Some of it I sell to local businesses. Electricity's so expensive and they're able to use this to keep the lights on and everything running. It's cheaper than their gas and electric bill. The only thing they need is a conversion box, which I also happily sell them." Archer gestured over to a far wall. Alvin saw things that looked like old radios piled up. "Concentrated, the skins are highly explosive."

"So, what? You sell some of it to the military, too?"

"No. I tried, but they weren't interested. I make my own bombs."

"Why?"

"Because I'm going to blow up the Point."

For the first time since watching him drink the rabbit's blood, Alvin thought that, maybe, Archer was completely fucking crazy.

"You're going to blow it up?"

"Yeah. See, I'm going to shuck this rade and put his skin in that little bombshell there." Alvin looked at the canthing. "I have a lot more of them. Get enough of these little bombs together and they'll have the impact of an atomic bomb. I've got an airplane in a hangar out at the airstrip on the edge of town. I'm going to take a bunch of these babies up in the air and drop 'em right down on the Point."

Archer had now clipped all the rade's fingertips off. He pulled a pair of metal tongs from the barrel and went about picking up the needle-like fingertips and dropping them into the bomb casing. Alvin didn't want to be here anymore. He thought Archer might be able to help him but Alvin didn't know if it was worth it. Alvin thought the night had turned on Archer. Maybe he had been a good person at one point in his life but something had happened and he had become something else. A lunatic. A would-be terrorist. A palpable sense of death enshrouded Archer and the Shucking Room. Alvin was frightened and depressed. To stay here, he felt, was even more soul deadening than working at the Point.

"This is all... fascinating," Alvin began, "but I think I really need to go."

"There's nowhere to go."

"I can't help but think there is. Maybe you could just tell me how to get to the address."

"I'll show you. I'll show you all kinds of things."

"You're busy and I'm in a hurry. If you could just give me a roundabout idea of how to get there, I'll leave you alone and go check it out."

"You'll get nowhere."

"Please give me the key to get out."

"I can't do that."

"Why not?"

"Because you're going to help me drop the bombs."

"I can't help you do that. I don't think I necessarily agree with what happens at the Point either, but I can't help you blow it up."

"Yes. You will. You don't really have a choice. We'll destroy the Point, get some fucking *daylight* back, let people get their *lives* back, and then we'll all live happily ever after. Isn't that what you want? It's your moral obligation to help me do this."

"I don't think it's a good idea."

"Trust me. Until we blow up the Point, there's nothing for you out there. You'll wander around at night. You won't even remember the day. You won't be able to get back into your house. You know why? Because the Point has sent a representative there to take your place. A simulacrum. That's what they're using the skin for. Not the rade skin but the human skin. The baby skin. That's why the abortion clinic has to run all night. So they can harvest more skin. I've seen 'em do it. Take truckloads of that skin up to the Point. And then they make simulacra out of those skins. I bet you and your wife couldn't have any kids, could ya? What good is a non-productive member of society? No good at all. The Point has to invest in the future. Your simulacrum has probably been in there fucking your wife for longer than you know. But the society can't have too many kids. What it needs is more workers. Hence the abortions…"

Alvin slowly made his way to the barrel of tools. There was a metal bar in there. He imagined Archer using it to roll up the skins of the rades and wondered how far off the mark he was.

A lot of what Archer said made sense. Alvin could see it. He could see it all happening. It sounded exactly like the type of thing the Point would do. But he couldn't agree to help blow it up. Not on Archer's suspicion and hearsay. He needed to get back in his house. Maybe he needed to go back to the police station to find out what happened to people like Lars. Maybe he needed to find this abortion clinic. See if what Archer said was true. But he wasn't going to do anything against his will. He wasn't going to be held hostage by this madman.

"Tell you what," Alvin said. "Let me go. Let me explore a little bit. If I can't find this address, if I can't get back into my house, I'll come back, okay? What'll I have to lose?"

Archer sighed and dropped the tongs in the barrel. He turned to look at the rade.

"You don't understand," he said.

"Understand what?"

"That you are nothing. I am the only living thing here. Is that not obvious to you? You're as good as dead. This is where you go to die. You have no more life. No more spirit. Here, your physical body can die and you can be irradiated and become one of them. There is no way out. You're lost and you're never going to find your way home again. This is the blackest fucking rabbit hole you could possibly fall down. Everyone is dead. Everyone is asleep. The destruction of the Point is the only thing that can bring life back to this city. I am the only one who can resurrect them. You should understand that. You were chosen for this. You followed me here. I haven't made you do anything."

Alvin hit him. He was mad. He didn't even think about it. He nailed him in the back of the head with the bar. Archer went forward but he didn't go out. The bar made a loud clanging sound and vibrated viciously. He almost dropped it.

"Give me the key," Alvin said.

"I can't do that."

Alvin hauled the bar back and hit him on the top of his head. This time he felt the clang all the way up to his elbows. Archer quickly grabbed an arrow and thrust it toward Alvin. It caught him in the left arm and he knew he had to move fast before he took another one. He took a giant roundhouse swing with the bar, catching Archer in the back of the neck. His head snapped back and he went down onto his knees then fell forward until he was on all fours. Blood poured from his head and onto the gleaming cement floor. Alvin reached down and put his hand in his pocket, feeling the keys and yanking them out.

"I saved your life," Archer said. "And this is the payment."

"You're fucking insane."

"I'll find you." Alvin walked quickly to the door. "I have nothing better to do. You know that, don't you? I'm going to find you and feed you to the rades piece by fucking piece."

With shaky hands, Alvin undid the lock. He threw the bar back into the Shucking Room. It landed on Archer's back and bounced off, clanging loudly on the floor. He thought about throwing the keys too, but decided to pocket them. Archer had declared war and Alvin didn't want to give him any advantages. From the outside, he pulled the door closed and noticed there was the same type of padlock there too. He snapped it shut and continued down the dark alleyway.

A Hospital at Night
Part Eight

April coughed out cigarette smoke and coughed out the night and walked back into the too bright lobby of the hushed hospital and into the elevator that felt like a tomb and back up to Alvin's floor. The outside chill still clung to her and she kept Mirabel's sweater pulled tight around her shoulders. She harbored a secret desire to walk into Alvin's room and find nurses and Doctor Banks gathered around him, trying to revive him. Instead she found Mirabel seated in one of the two chairs beside the bed.

"How is he?" April asked.

"Same."

April sat down in the chair next to her.

"Thanks for the cigarette. I borrowed your sweater."

"Don't worry about it. Are you planning on going back home?"

April chuffed out a laugh.

"A hotel, maybe? You could probably even take a little nap here. You have to be tired."

"I couldn't sleep. I wouldn't want to wake up."

Mirabel nodded. "I'm here to listen, if you want me to

be."

"You know, I don't think I really hated him until I found out he was cheating on me."

"Are you sure about that?"

"A wife knows. Wouldn't you know it if your husband was cheating on you?"

"Definitely. I could tell just by looking at him."

"Well, he had become someone else so I wouldn't have been able to tell just by looking at him. But he would come home after one of his mysterious absences and I could smell her on him."

"Did you ever confront him about it?"

"I couldn't. Saying it out loud would have just made it more real, if that makes any sense. But I wouldn't sleep with him after I knew, not that he really wanted it anyway. Guess he didn't need it. I don't think it makes me a better person or anything, but I would never have slept with Morning if I didn't know Al was cheating on me. And the worst part of him doing something like that was how it made me look to other people. Apparently, he didn't really try to keep it a secret. I ran into a neighbor at the store and she looked at me like she didn't know me and I asked her what was wrong and she said she thought I had changed the color of my hair. And then she started to explain and then she stopped and there was this moment of realization. We both knew. She had seen Alvin out with someone else and assumed it was me. She didn't have to say anything else."

"I'm sure it hurts."

"It's one of the worst feelings in the world. And it's amazing how I could manage to explain away everything else—maybe he lost his job because he was depressed and wasn't able to make it in on time or fulfill his duties while he was there, maybe he started using drugs to cope with the depression, maybe he really *was* just bored and needed a change—but I couldn't find any way to justify him fucking someone else. I gave him everything. And what he wanted was something new."

She started crying again. These were painful things she was saying but they needed to be said. She cried and listened to the beeping and felt Mirabel's hand on her leg and she wanted to die. To die or run back out to the night and get lost and never come back.

Eight

Alvin proceeded down the alley, going back toward his house, knowing it was useless. He kept a watch out for the rades. The one rade Archer had killed was no longer in the yard. Now Alvin found it curious, since Archer seemed to have such a vested interest in the rades, why he hadn't taken this one for himself. Maybe he didn't want the burden of carrying it. Maybe he was afraid Alvin would think it was strange and refuse to follow him into his Shucking Room.

He looked up at the sky, trying to find the moon, stars, something, anything to let him know he was still on the same planet. But the only things to remind him of that were the silent houses all around. What was he going to do? He couldn't just wander around in this perpetual night for the rest of his life. That was ridiculous. He needed answers. He needed to get back to April.

He reached the end of the alley and to his right, his house. What used to be his house? Now he didn't really know what to call it. He walked up through the yard. He couldn't let himself believe things had become as strange as they seemed. Something had to have happened to April. There was no way she could believe this man in their house was him. Maybe at first glance... Or maybe they had just grown that far apart. He didn't really see how it was possible. They were the happiest couple he knew. They still managed to spend a little time together. Maybe they were just too used to each other. Maybe it was all a joke. Maybe the replacement was some new lover. But that didn't explain anything else. The weird night police. The endless night. Fucking Archer and the rades. The Acme Demolition crew still on the top of his house.

They now had nearly the entire thing covered in wires. He wondered how much time he had left. Why would they want to blow up his house? Why had they already blown up so many of the other houses? It just didn't make any sense.

He walked up through his backyard and climbed the wooden steps of the porch. These were all things he had done hundreds of times. He reached the porch and turned around, looking out over the yard, trying to put things into perspective. The grass needed mowing again. How much time had passed? It felt like it couldn't have been much more than a couple of days but the way the grass looked, he would have to guess it had been nearly a week. Other than the grass, everything was the same. The houses on the other side of Thistle. The neighbors' garage just across the alley.

He turned back around and crossed the few feet of the porch until he once again stood in front of the door. He touched the knob and turned it, just to make sure. It was locked. Of course it was. The thought of breaking and entering once again crossed his mind but so did the thought of going back to the police station. He had already been processed, he didn't want to think what would happen to him now.

Reluctantly, he crossed the yard, going back toward the

alley. His mouth felt very dry. He stuck his finger into his mouth and poked his tongue. It was so dry it didn't even feel like a tongue. His head and cheek throbbed. His left arm hurt from where Archer had stuck him with the arrow. He felt paranoid and on edge. A rade could be lurking anywhere. While they weren't the quickest things in the world, he didn't know if he had the energy or the strength to outrun one. His house could potentially blow up at any minute, although he thought the demolition crew would probably have to get off the roof before they did that. But he felt like he was supposed to be doing something. Something to stop his house from being blown up but he couldn't think what that might be.

He would continue on to downtown. Maybe he would find other people downtown. Someone more like Ben and less like Archer. Someone who could help him stop the people wiring up his house. He poked his tongue again, coughed and gagged. It unleashed a bit of saliva and, at that moment, all he wanted was a drink of water.

As he walked down the alley and got ready to step on the sidewalk, something hit him from the left. He felt hot breath in his ear and a hand on his cock.

"You have to fuck me," the voice said.

He grabbed the individual molesting him by her upper arms and thrust her away, still holding onto her. It was a young woman, probably not much older than a teenager. She had a black faux hawk, multiple piercings, and looked like she dressed from the rack at the mall store that tried to be edgy but was still a mall store.

She slipped a hand under her tartan skirt and massaged herself. "Come on," she said. "We can do it right here. Nobody'll notice."

"Jesus. Calm down."

"No. You don't understand. I need it. I have to have it."

Alvin had never been in a situation like this. He knew he wasn't going to do anything with her but he didn't really know how to tell her 'no' either. He thought about just turning and running in the other direction but maybe he could get this person to help him.

"If you don't calm down," he said, "I can't give you what you want."

This seemed to placate her somewhat. She took her hand out of her crotch and asked hopefully, "So, you'll fuck me?"

"We'll see. But later, okay? I need some help first."

"Whatever."

He took his hands from her arms. "Are you a night person too?"

"I wouldn't be here if I wasn't."

"Did you work for the Point?"

"Um, in a roundabout way."

"You seem awfully young."

"For some things."

"What did you do?"

"I worked in one of their stores as a model."

"They have stores?"

"They own all the stores in Dayton."

"How long have you been here?"

"I have no idea. Look, you don't have to talk to me or anything. I'll just lean against this wall and you can fuck me, okay? It'll be quick. You can't wear a condom though. Don't worry, I don't have any diseases or anything. And then I'll be on my way and you can be on yours. How's that sound?"

"Besides crazy? Well, let's see. First of all, I'm married and I love my wife."

"Okay. Okay. You'll never see your wife again but okay."

"Second, I don't know you."

"Does it matter? Are you saying you wouldn't fuck me?"

"That's beside the point. Third, I have things I have to do."

"Like what? There's nothing to do here. You just fucking wander around until you go into a coma and then you die. Might as well fuck it up while you can."

"That's a lovely sentiment, it really is, but I'm afraid I'm not that defeated yet."

"That's refreshing, I guess." At this, she began fingering her nipple through her shirt. It was apparent she wasn't wearing a bra. Alvin reached out his hand to bat hers away and she grabbed it and put it on her breast. He could feel her nipple pressing into his palm. He couldn't remember the last time he'd had sex. He was aroused but would never admit it. He yanked his hand away.

"Stop, okay. Just stop. I'll never give you what you want if you keep doing that."

He put his hands in his pockets and thought this might be the most retarded conversation he'd ever had in his life.

"Okay, fine," she said. "You mentioned some things you have to do. What kinds of things? I can tell you why they're stupid and why you should be fucking me instead."

Alvin poked his tongue again and looked back at his house.

"You see them people up there?"

"Yeah. That's the demo crew. It means you've been

scheduled for an outage."

"An outage?"

"It's a nicer way of saying detonation."

"I think there's been some mistake. My house should not be detonated. For one, my wife is still in there."

The girl scoffed. "They'll evacuate everyone before they detonate it."

"My wife is in there with another man."

"Then why don't you fuck *me*. That'll teach her."

Alvin laughed distantly and jabbed his tongue again, this time with the index finger of both hands. "You don't understand. She thinks that other man is me. He's a..." He had to think of the word. "A simulacrum."

"I don't know what the fuck that word means."

"It's like someone who looks kind of like me. Someone who's meant to take the place of me. That's what they do at the Point. They make these things with other people's flesh... and I think they use the flesh from abortions, too."

"They do something with them. That's why they pay good money. That's why I need you to fuck me."

Alvin jabbed at his tongue harder this time. Now he thought he tasted blood in the back of his throat. "So you want me to cheat on my wife and have sex with you so that you can get pregnant and get an abortion."

She nodded. "That sounds about right."

"No way."

"You do it and I can tell you how to keep your house from getting blown up."

He dug into his pocket and pulled out the address, unfolded it, and pressed it very close to her face. "Do you know where this is?"

He saw some sense of recognition flicker in her eyes but

it was immediately replaced by the cold eyes of a predator. "Fuck me and I'll tell you where it is."

Alvin sucked some blood back into his throat and watched his house as the workers continued dropping those wires off the roof.

The girl grabbed his hand and said, "Let's take a little walk and give you a chance to think about it."

Alvin took one last, longing glance back at his house and said, "Okay."

"Okay you'll do me?"

"I don't know about all that yet. I need to find one of the sleepers. Do you know where I can find one of them?"

"They're all over. It shouldn't be very hard. Why do you need to find one of them?"

"There's something I find fascinating about them."

"You don't act like someone who's in much of a hurry."

"No. I am. Time is very much of the essence, but I have to know."

"Have to know what?"

"What the sleepers are."

"They're just people."

"People don't sleep all the time. It's not right."

She rolled her eyes and pulled him along. They began walking down Payne Avenue, trying the doors on all the houses they passed. They were all locked. They exchanged names. When she told him her name was May he laughed and said, "That's cute."

"Glad you like my name," she said.

"No. It's just that... my wife's name is April. April. May."

"Well, I guess when you're finished fucking me you'll move on to June."

He didn't say anything to that. He could imagine it happening and the prospect seemed terrifying.

"You look like you've been in a fight."

Alvin explained his wounds to her—his forehead, his cheek, his arm. She told him she knew who Archer was and that she had never trusted police. When he asked her why she told him she had her reasons. He told her to make sure to keep a lookout for rades. She said she never stopped looking out for them and she knew how to take care of herself. "I'm not new to this lifestyle."

Alvin wasn't sure what lifestyle she meant.

Eventually, about the tenth house down, they came to a duplex that had one unlocked door. Alvin walked in cautiously, figuring the house would either be filled with rades or sleeping people. Or, possibly even night people.

Alvin flipped on lights as he passed through the lower floor of the house. They all seemed too bright even though they didn't seem to work very well. A lot of them flickered as though they were in the middle of a massive thunderstorm and the power was getting ready to go out or like they hadn't been screwed in all the way. Maybe the wiring was just old. Bright and flickering, worming their way behind his eyes and swimming around in his brain. He felt nauseous. He realized he had been holding May's hand since she had grabbed it in front of his house. He pulled his hand away, feeling her sweat on his palm.

"Fine," she said. "I didn't want to hold your hand anyway."

"I gotta…" The floor swam beneath Alvin like the house was rocking back and forth on the sea. "I gotta look through this place."

"You'll want to hurry up. The crew isn't going to spend

forever wiring up your house. And you still have to fuck me. I bet it takes you a long time to come. You look like someone who has to fuck forever before anything happens. You look like the kind of person who doesn't even enjoy it. Like you'd be a million miles away when what most men want is wrapped right there around you."

She put her hands on his shoulders.

He shrugged them off.

"We could do it right here if you want to."

"Not... Not if there are any sleepers here."

Alvin began looking through the house, flipping on more lights as he went. There weren't any bedrooms on the first floor. Alvin began climbing the steps to the second floor. May stayed downstairs.

"Aren't you coming?"

"No. I'm gonna stay down here. Those things give me the creeps."

"What things? People?"

"When they're asleep like that... Knowing they're always like that. It makes me think they're dead."

"Suit yourself."

"Unless you're going to take me up there and fuck my brains out. Then I'll come with you."

Alvin didn't say anything. He continued climbing.

He reached the top of the stairs and opened the first door on his right. There was a lump beneath the covers on the bed. Alvin crossed the room. A man's fat and balding head stuck out from the top of the covers. Alvin sat down on the edge of the bed. He nudged the strange sleeping man. He could see why they gave May the creeps. He shook him but the man didn't wake up. He buried his first two fingers in the folds of the man's neck until he found a pulse. It was strong and steady. He definitely wasn't dead.

Alvin inspected his fingers. The tips of his first two fingers were discolored. It looked like dried blood. He smelled them. They smelled coppery. Dried blood or rust. Maybe it was from his tongue. He could still taste the blood in his mouth. Maybe one of his head wounds had reopened. He touched the small hole in his left arm. His fingers came away wet. It was still bleeding. But it didn't hurt very badly. He wiped his fingers on the front of his shirt.

"Wake up." Alvin shook the body harder. Hard enough to make the man's fat lips jiggle against his gums.

"Come on, you fat fuck. Wake up!"

Still nothing. Maybe the sleepers were more than just asleep. Maybe they were in some type of coma. Alvin climbed up on the bed, straddling the man. He began jumping up and down, chanting, "Wake up! Wake up! Wake up!" He kept bouncing long after the point any normal human would have been awake. He studied the sleeping man's face the entire time.

Disheartened, he stopped jumping and got off the bed. The lights flickered and Alvin planted his hands on the bed to steady himself. He coughed. The taste of blood was stronger. He rummaged around in the nightstands. Amongst many objects he did not like to imagine this man owning, Alvin found a black cigarette lighter. He threw back the covers on the bed. He went to the foot of the bed, flicked the lighter, and held the flame to the bottom of the man's grossly calloused foot.

The man's foot twitched. Alvin looked at his face. The man opened his eyes. The lighter went out. The man's eyes were closed again. Alvin did it again. The same thing happened, only this time he felt something. It was similar to what he had felt back at the police station. Some connection to another world. The old world? *His* old world? Like the room he was sitting on went all swimmy. He thought again of the image of the house rocking on a strange sea. He looked at the bottom of the man's foot. There was now a blister there, burned slightly black from the lighter. Alvin held the lighter to his other foot, careful to pay close attention this time. He flicked the lighter. The man's foot twitched again. And, this time, when his eyes opened, Alvin felt nothing. Or, rather, he felt some sense of... yearning. He imagined an alarm clock going off in the distance. Birds chirping. The scents of coffee brewing and bacon frying. The squeal of school bus brakes.

He reeled with desire.

Sliding the lighter into his pocket, he went back to the head of the bed. He bent down and pulled the man's eyelids open. He stared in fascination. The man's eyes had rusted. Flakes of rust were caught up in the eyelashes and created deposits at the corners of the man's eyes. Alvin pulled his fingers away and looked at the tips. They looked the same as they had before only now he was sure it was rust. He put his fingers back into the fat of the man's neck. He couldn't find a pulse this time. But he could feel the rust like dried sweat. He struggled to roll the man over, yanking off the covers. His shirt and pajama bottoms had been partially eaten away. In the holes, where flesh should have been, was more rust. Much of it had flaked off into the bed. The lights flickered and the room rocked around him. He turned and left the bedroom without flipping the lights off. This man had gone to sleep. He had closed his eyes a long time ago and then he had turned to rust. Alvin wondered how something like that could happen. He wondered what something like that could possibly mean, if anything. He had seen the man open his eyes only moments before and, while he couldn't recall the color, he knew they had not been made of rust. Perhaps Alvin had done this to the man. Perhaps his presence had made the man turn to rust. That was ridiculous, of course, he told himself. He went down the stairs as quickly as possible. He wanted to be as far away from the sleeping man as possible. He coughed and sucked blood down his throat. He fought the urge to shiver. If he shivered just once, he was afraid he wouldn't be able to stop.

May sat on a couch in the family room, leafing through a magazine. She sat with her legs parted, her white underwear plainly visible.

"I saw you look," she said. "You want some? We could do it right here on the couch."

Alvin was distracted. He threw one last look at the stairway, as though the rusted man might have gotten up from the bed and come lumbering after him.

"So? Whaddya say?" May pointed between her legs.

"You know, when you just *give* it away, it's much less appealing."

"Whatever. Guys don't care." She crossed her legs. "There. Now do you want to?"

He shook his head in disbelief.

"So, did you find out what it was you wanted to find out?"

"I... don't know. He was *rusting*."

"I told you the sleepers were creepy fucking bastards. Now you'll believe me. See, I'm not new at this. I know what I'm doing. And I *will* be able to help you."

"Come on," he said. "We need to get going."

"To my apartment?"

"Is your apartment downtown?"

"It just so happens that it is."

"Okay then. We can go there."

"And?"

"And what?"

"You said."

"I didn't promise anything. I'm sure we'll pass someone along the way. You can drag them in an alley and have your way with them or whatever. I'll even wait for you."

"Geez, that makes me feel pretty special."

"When did you give up?"

She stood up from the couch, tossed the magazine back in her place.

"What do you mean?"

"When did you stop trying?"

"When I realized everything was useless."

"But, if you've never really tried, how can you be so sure?"

"Have you tried to go back home?"

"Yes. I told you that."

"And what happened?"

"The first time I was arrested. And then my simulacrum beat me up. I almost got attacked by a rade. Another time the door was locked."

"And you didn't break in?"

"No."

"Why not?"

"I didn't want to get arrested again."

"See. So you've really given up too."

"No, I haven't. I'm trying to find another way."

"Really? Because, let me tell you, those guys up there on your roof? They're not just fucking around. Your house is going to be detonated and then everything you know, everything that's been slipping away from you? Gone. Just like that. And while you should be fucking me so I can tell you how you might be able to stop that, you're just dicking around. Wasting time. Know why? Because you know it's useless. You know there isn't going to be any going back to your house, no getting your wife back."

"Then why should I do what you want so you can tell me how to do that? Why do that if it's useless?"

"Hope. I can tell you how and then you can have hope. Uselessness is one thing. Hopelessness is another. When you've lost all hope… then you'll be just like me. There are always exceptions. Maybe you'll be the exception. You can tell yourself that, can't you?"

Alvin raised his hands, turned so his palms faced him. They were both covered in the rust residue. "I think I have to. Come on."

She stood up from the couch. He opened the front door and stepped out onto the porch. He heard a loud sound to his left and snapped his head in that direction. An arrow had pierced the doorframe, stuck into the wood at least an inch. The arrow pierced a note.

"What is it?" May asked, leaning over his shoulder, snaking a hand around to the front of his pants.

"A note."

"Duh. I can see that. What's it say?"

"'The hunt is on.'"

"What's that mean?"

"It means we're in a lot of trouble."

"Someone after you?"

"Yeah. Archer."

"We could stick to the alleys all the way downtown if

you want to."

"No. I think he's pretty familiar with the alleys. We'll just go down Payne until we get downtown. Keep an eye out. If you see any movement at all, we'll have to hide."

"Roger."

Cautiously, they crept down the walk of the house until they reached the sidewalk and turned back downtown. They crossed a narrow side street and heard a sound to their right. Alvin looked into the alley and saw a glowing rade. It was crouched down over a body. The rade turned its head in their direction and Alvin saw the milky glow of its eyes.

"Let's walk faster," he said.

They reached downtown in what felt like ten minutes. It was all downhill so the walking was relatively easy. May pointed out her apartment. It was a loft that had been converted from an old warehouse at the very end of Payne. Across the street from her apartment was a building. Besides the police station, it was possibly one of the only places he had seen that had more than one or two lights on. There was a line of cars backed out onto Main Street and continuing toward the city center. Not everyone was in a car. Some people just stood there in line. They were all girls and women, various ages.

"What's that?" Alvin asked.

"That's Mr. Lucky's Abortion Clinic. It used to be a Chinese restaurant."

She grabbed him by the hand and led him up to her apartment. Alvin held the curtain open and looked out at the abortion clinic. "So that's where all the people are?"

"Just the women."

"Why?"

"Why not?"

"I'm not anti-abortion or anything but that just seems... ghoulish. So they just... what? Drive up there and go in and get an abortion and then go back out?"

"Oh, they don't even have to go in. Well, I mean, there is a little room there if you don't have a car but most of them are performed right there in the car."

"And what happens to the uh..."

"Fetuses?"

"Yeah."

"I'm not sure. I think it has something to do with the Point."

"Everything does. So you're one of them?"

"Don't say it like that. 'Them.' It sounds so condescending."

"What is it? Drugs?"

"Money. Maybe sometimes for drugs. This whole town is corrupt and I don't think we're the only one. The Point owns everything. They have files on everyone. You get a job and then you lose your job or you quit, you can't get work. I could whore myself but what's that? A little here and a little there. Just enough to barely keep me alive. Dr. Lucky's pays good money for its abortions. I can live for a year off what they pay me."

"It seems illegal."

"What's legal? The police force is the biggest drug cartel we have here. If they look the other way when it comes to something like abortion selling or prostitution, then it means those people have more money to buy drugs from them. It's all a circle. Like a circle of death. So if you don't want to give me what I need, then I'll just go find someone else and forget all about you. But if you think I'm going to tell you how you can stop them from detonating your house then you can go fuck yourself."

Alvin closed the curtains. He wished he had more walls to put between himself and the abortion clinic. Himself and the whole city. May had mentioned something about hopelessness and he felt it reaching out from her. He felt it coming from her. Was he her hope? Even if it was a sad, desperate, sickening kind of hope? What harm would it do anyway? He was sterile but May didn't have to know that. If he told her he was sterile she would just think he was lying to get out of it. April was quite possibly cheating on him. He couldn't remember the last time he had had sex. May was very attractive. No one would have to know. He had never seen May before this evening. He would probably never see her again. He was running out of time. There was no way he could make it back to April unless he did this with May. Did he want to make it back to April? He thought he did but maybe what he really wanted to make it back to was knowledge. If he could prevent them from blowing his house up, he could buy himself some more time. He could get some things sorted out. Everything had become so jumbled up and confused. Everything wanted to reach into his skull and take little bites out of his brains.

May stood in front of him, nearly crying, breathing heavily. She had taken off her boots. Her toenails were painted black. Alvin pushed her back on the bed.

"You're like a fucking succubus," he said.

She looked at him with big brown eyes, her arms raised above her head, offering herself to him, her knees bent over the edge of the bed. He went down on his knees between her legs. He pushed her skirt up. She wore white hip hugger panties. He opened his mouth and bit down on her pubic mound. Not hard. He chewed softly. She squirmed and moaned. He unfastened the buckle at the side of her skirt and slid it off. He continued grinding his teeth against her, moving his hands under her ass, under her panties, moving his fingertips along her anus. His penis was stiff and uncomfortable in his pants. He wanted to taste her. He couldn't remember how long it had been since he had tasted April, since he had given April pleasure. He stripped off May's underwear. There was a tiny patch of pubic hair above her sex. He pulled her apart with his thumbs and plunged his tongue into her. Her wetness coated his lips and his tongue. He sucked it into his mouth and it mixed with the blood taste and he drank it down like a cocktail. He closed his lips around her clitoris and sucked on it. She squealed and grabbed the back of his head and pulled him up. He stripped off her shirt and pulled off his own while she expertly undid the button and zipper of his pants. She pulled his pants and underwear down to his knees. His erection bobbed in front of her face. She ran her tongue along the underside and took the head into her mouth. He grabbed the back of her head and pulled her toward him until she gagged. He didn't stop. He thrust against her. She squeezed his balls and he could feel her gagging throat against the head of his penis. He nearly came.

He pulled her off him and threw her back on the bed. She spread her legs and reached her hand down to her cunt and pulled herself open for him. He shoved it in fully on the first thrust. Her eyes rolled back in her head. He lowered his head and bit one of her nipples. Bit it harder. Pounded against her. She clawed his chest. She put his hands around her throat. She smacked him in the face when he didn't squeeze. He squeezed gently. She punched him in the forehead. He could feel it split open. Blood dripped down onto her chest and gathered at the end of his nose as he continued to pound against her. He squeezed her throat until the veins at her temples began to bulge. She grabbed his upper arms and bucked wildly against him. He could feel her vagina squeezing him, her legs wrapped around his ass, pulling him into her. They were both covered in blood and the stink of it filled the room. She removed her hands from his arms and dug them both into his chest. He could feel his skin pop beneath her fingernails. He wrapped his hands around her hips, now wanting nothing more than to ram her as hard as possible, batter her insides, break her. He thrust against her, their skin smacking together, locked into one another with ropes of blood and smeared come and fingernails and then she cried out and didn't stop and he let go inside of her, working himself as deep as he could possibly go.

He rolled off her and lay to her left, his muscles shaking.

"Wow," she said.

"Tell me. You promised." He wondered if he should tell her if he was sterile and then thought better of it. Now he had cheated on April and, in a way, he was cheating May.

"Come on. Don't you wanna stick around? Get cleaned up?"

"I need to go. You told me you would tell me. You told me you would help me."

May sighed deeply. "Let's take a shower. I feel disgusting."

"No."

"What was the address again?"

Alvin leaned off the bed and fished his pants up off the floor. He pulled the rumpled piece of paper out of his pocket and flattened it out as best as possible. "1333 Ohio

Drive."

"And you don't know where that is?"

"I've never heard of it. I'm terrible with directions."

"It's two streets over from you." She explained to him where it was compared to his house.

"Why didn't we just go there when we were by the house?"

"Because you wouldn't agree to help me. You had several chances. I told you you could fuck me in the yard. I told you you could fuck me in the creepy sleeper's house. You didn't want to. Your choice."

"And how is this going to help me keep my house from getting detonated?"

"I don't know if it is. I didn't give you the piece of paper. I have no idea what you'll find there."

"So how do I keep my house from being detonated?"

"Well, for starters, you need to make sure it isn't supposed to be blown up. You said you lived there with your wife. It's possible she scheduled the detonation. The detonations are all ordered by the Point. You have to go there and fill out some paperwork."

"That's it?"

"They make it very hard. Do you have any ID on you?"

"No. I left it at the station."

"They'll want that."

"I can't get that."

"Look, you asked me to tell you how to stop your house from being detonated and I did that. The people at the Point are the only people who can call it off. I can't do it for you."

"Will you go with me?"

"I'd really like to get cleaned up first."

"We don't have time. Don't you understand that? Doesn't anybody understand that? I have *no time*."

"I have a car. Will that help?"

"Yes, that would help immensely."

"We can take it if I can take a shower first."

"Fine."

"You should take one too."

He did feel disgusting. A shower might feel nice. "Fine."

She stood up and he followed her into the bathroom. Looking at the small apartment as they passed through it, he could see that it was in total and complete disarray. She turned the water on and they got in the shower. He kept his back turned to her. Now that he had given her what she wanted, he felt repulsed by her. Repulsed by her agenda. He thought what she was doing was lower than fucking people for money. The scalding water stung his wounds. The soap stung them even more. The smell of the shampoo made him feel a little better about things. Then she turned off the water and he felt wrung out and exhausted. Like he could crawl back in the bed and sleep for days. He couldn't remember the last time he had slept but, since he also couldn't remember the last time he had seen daylight, he thought he had to have slept at some point. People don't just blackout during the day. She rummaged through some clothes on the floor and found a pair of jeans and a green t-shirt with Che Guevara's head on it. Alvin put his dirty clothes back on. He didn't think she would have anything to fit him.

"I hope the car starts," she said.

"What do you mean?"

"I haven't driven it in a while. People like to steal gas

and I don't have any kind of lock on the tank."

"Great. You know, if Archer gets a clear shot at me, he isn't going to miss. I need the car for a shield as much as anything."

"Let's hope it starts then." She plucked a ring of keys from a holder beside the door and went out into the hallway. Alvin followed. She tossed the keys to Alvin. They bounced off his chest and clattered to the floor. "Good catch."

He followed her down the darkened stairway. She pulled the door to her building open and the next thing Alvin saw was the point of an arrow only a couple inches from his heart. It had gone through her throat. He caught her under the arms before she could collapse. Another arrow, just the very tip, punched through the back of her skull. That one must have gone through her eye. Alvin ran out to the sidewalk, toward the only car he saw there, using her body as a shield and feeling bad about it. He didn't even take the time to see where Archer might have been shooting from. For right now, he just wanted inside the car. If it didn't go with the set of keys he had, at least he would be behind steel and glass and able to lock the doors if they were unlocked in the first place. He pulled the door open and felt lucky. He slid behind the wheel, dropping May's corpse out onto the street, and slammed the door shut. He clutched the wheel, his hands shaking. Archer had flown two arrows. The first had gone through her jugular. The second had gone through her eye and then her brain. The first shot would have killed her if the arrow was removed, unleashing a torrent of blood. The second arrow probably killed her on impact. The Archer didn't miss. He had shot as soon as the building door was opened. If Alvin had gone first, he would be dead.

Morning is Dead

He almost wished he had. Then all this would be over.

He put the key in the ignition and turned. It was the right key. The car sputtered and he gave it some gas and it roared to life. He rolled away from the curb and saw Archer wandering back up Payne Avenue, out in the open. Maybe he hadn't stuck around long enough to see that Alvin was dead. Maybe he had such faith in his work that he didn't think he needed to. Pomposity was just one more reason for Alvin to hate Archer. If he didn't end this now, he would have it hanging over his head the entire time. He had enough things to think about. He still didn't know if he should go to this address or if he should just travel on to the Point. Ben had called it a safe house or something. Maybe they made fake IDs or detonation desist orders.

Alvin turned onto Payne and gunned the accelerator. Archer ducked into an alley on the left. Alvin turned the car to the left and sped down the alley.

Archer jumped a chainlink fence to his right. Alvin ran the car into the fence. It tore it down with relative ease.

Archer was now on the wooden porch of a house. Alvin gunned the accelerator one final time and flew into the porch. The car smashed and shattered against it but did a good deal of damage to the porch. Archer stood in front of the car. Alvin could see him very clearly because the windshield was broken out. Archer had his bow in his hands and an arrow nocked but he couldn't draw his arm back far enough because it was pinned against the house. Alvin threw himself to his left, out of the car, hitting the glass-and wood-covered ground. An arrow landed just to his left. It was a weak shot, the arrow barely penetrating the soil. If Archer were able to see him and draw a correct shot, he wouldn't have missed. Once again, Alvin felt pretty lucky.

He searched around on the ground until he came to a large sliver of wood from one of the porch railings. Maybe it would work.

It didn't. The second he stood up, an arrow pierced the hand holding the piece of wood and he dropped it. Then he collapsed to the ground again but not before he had a chance to see that Archer was still pinned.

Think.

Another arrow landed nearby. From nearly beneath the car, Alvin scanned the wreckage of the porch. He smelled something he thought was just the gassy scent of the car. But the more he smelled it, the more it smelled different. Like propane from a grill. He looked harder. Everything was so dark and twisted up it was hard to see. Then he saw it. A propane tank sitting in the twisted metal of the grill. Further back, he saw Archer's foot on the underside of the porch. The bastard was trapped. He wasn't going anywhere without amputating his foot.

Alvin took off his shirt and wrapped it around one of the pieces of wood. He still had the lighter he had used on the sleeper. He pulled it from his pocket and quickly lit it. He touched the flame to the shirt until it was blazing and then tossed it toward the porch. As soon as he heard the initial *whoosh* he took off back toward the alley. He still had faith in Archer's shooting ability so he just kept running. Turning around might mean taking an arrow in the eye.

A Hospital at Night
Part Nine

Mirabel had to leave to make her rounds. April sat in the chair and thought about funeral parlors. She was very tired. She had been awake for a very long time, the day starting relatively banal and ending in catastrophe. Ending in something she wasn't even sure she had pieced together just yet. She wondered if it was wrong to wish Alvin would remain in a coma the rest of her life. Of course it was wrong. But, if he remained in a coma then she wouldn't have to deal with the guilt of his death or with him. She didn't think she could deal with him anymore. She hadn't been able to deal with him for a long time. She knew her love was supposed to be unconditional, but she didn't think hers was. Sometimes she thought love was the only thing she had to give and, therefore, was the only thing she could take away. She felt wrung out and exhausted. Maybe Mirabel was right. Maybe she should go check into a hotel and get some rest. Her being here wasn't doing Alvin any good. She didn't even want to be here. She felt like it was something she had to do. She had closed herself to Alvin a long time ago. It was sad. It was sad to admit that to herself, but it was the truth, a comfortable sadness. If it was up to her, if she didn't have to worry about anyone talking about how heartless she was, she would have left the hospital as soon as she found out Morning was dead. He was the one she loved. Alvin had become an inconvenience but it was an inconvenience she could never abandon, not completely. She felt herself begin to nod off and squeezed her arm. The pain snapped her awake.

Mirabel was back by her side.

"I feel like such a terrible person," April said.

"Why? Because you want him to die?"

April couldn't say yes. She looked at the mummy sprouting tubes and nodded her head.

"That doesn't make you crazy. It doesn't make you like him. You know, you spend enough of your life around crazy people and start to think you're crazy too. You start doubting everything and thinking every thought you ever had is wrong. My mom died from Alzheimer's a couple years back. She had been in a bad way for a long time before that. We moved her in with us and, eventually, we had to put her in a nursing home. I felt bad about it. It was one of the hardest things I had ever done. But there wasn't any other choice. And after she went into the nursing home, I begged God to take her, I *wanted* her to die. For her sake. For my sake. I didn't want to see someone suffer like that. And then she finally passed. So far gone she didn't even know I was standing right beside her when she took her last breath. But she talked. And she saw a lot of people. Old friends. Old family. All long since dead. Maybe they were just hallucinations, maybe she was glimpsing heaven, I don't know, but when she finally went, I was relieved. It felt like I had my life back. It wasn't complete anymore, not without her, but it was mine."

April was crying again.

"I didn't mean to make you cry." Mirabel patted her knee. "It's like this creepy movie my husband took me to see a few years back. It had this girl who lives in a trashy motel and she lets this man start staying with her. And he sees all these bugs, *aphids*, everywhere. On the walls. In the bed. Under his skin. It isn't long before she's seeing them too. By the end of the movie, I was convinced they were *every*where. Then, on the way home, you know what my husband said?"

April shook her head.

"He said, 'There wasn't a single bug in that movie. Them folks was just crazy.' He was right."

April laughed a small laugh. It felt good.

"Aw, I love you, Mirabel." She put her arm around the older woman's shoulder and the women laughed together.

A figure moved in front of the door, closing off the light from the hallway and plunging the room into almost total darkness.

Nine

Alvin stalked down the alley behind the house with the burning porch. He knew Archer wouldn't give him the satisfaction of screaming. That would let Alvin know he was alive and, when the screaming stopped, it would let Alvin know he was dead. His right hand bled profusely. He held it against the thigh of his pants as he trudged along. He was bare-chested and felt stupid. He didn't even like to take his shirt off at the beach. He supposed he could just break into one of the houses and raid their closets. That wasn't a bad idea. He didn't know what the hell he was doing anyway. He was lost. Everything seemed to be melting away from him. Inside and outside. Not just melting but fracturing into jagged pieces and then melting so the edges of all those sharp pieces were dulled and then they couldn't even cut you anymore. The definition of meaninglessness. He had a purpose. To get to the Point and file a petition or some paperwork or something but everything May had told him was already starting to break up. His purpose seemed like something his brain had to seize upon and struggle with so it didn't slip away.

Morning is Dead

From the alleyway, he came to a street he didn't know the name of. He walked up to the first house he came to. Besides being embarrassing, it was cold without a shirt. He could probably steal a sweater.

The porch creaked beneath Alvin. He put his hand on the doorknob and noticed the house number:

1333

He squinted at the street sign on the corner. He couldn't make it out. He stepped back off the porch and walked across the yard until he could read it. Ohio Drive. It seemed impossible. He thought May had told him it was a couple streets over from his house. He was blocks away from his house. It didn't make any sense. Did the street just move all over the city, disappearing and reappearing? He went back up to the porch and turned the knob. The door opened freely. It was dark inside. The sound of snoring came from behind one of the doors. That must be a bedroom. The man of the house would probably have a drawer full of t-shirts and a closet full of sweatshirts. Supposing there was a man of the house. He could probably find a leather jacket or puffy winter coat with some sports team's logo emblazoned on it. That was how people here dressed, like people just getting out of or going to prison. He opened the bedroom door. A couple lay in bed. Older. Alvin was secretly relieved by this. He had the fashion sense of an old man. Not that it mattered, he knew, but he still didn't want to have to dress like a clown.

He hadn't turned on any lights since coming into the house. He hadn't needed to. Maybe his eyes were adjusting to the darkness. Or maybe those flickering lights made him feel too weird. His mouth had gone dry again. He jabbed his tongue with his finger. He gagged and nearly vomited.

The room swam around him. He braced himself on a dresser and took some deep breaths. He was freezing and shivering. He needed to get a shirt on.

He pulled open a drawer. He grabbed the first white t-shirt he came to and put it on. It was pretty large. That didn't bother him. He went to the closet and opened it. It smelled like an old person. Moth balls, maybe? Was that the smell he always associated with the elderly? Something medicinal with just a trace of bowel or bladder issues. His stomach lurched without him being able to help it. He turned away from the closet and vomited onto the floor. It spattered up onto his pants. He could see chunks of it on his shoes. The smell and the sight of it made him vomit again. He dropped down onto his knees and vomited until he had nothing but dry heaves left. He wiped his mouth with the back of his right hand, slathering blood across his lips. He stood up slowly so the room wouldn't swirl around him again.

Focus. Focus, he told himself. Get a shirt and get to the Point. There wasn't anyone here who could help him. It was probably just a joke Benjamin was playing on him. It was probably something he did with all the inmates. Something to get their hopes up. Maybe something to give them hope like he had tried to do with May.

He turned back to the closet and sifted through the rack until he found a button down shirt, either dark blue, brown, or black. He couldn't tell in the dark. His night vision wasn't that good yet. He buttoned the shirt and decided he would go check the other closets of the house to see if he could find a winter coat. When he stepped out into the living room, he jumped.

A rade stood there, glowing in the darkness and sniffing

the air.

Fuck.

The rade turned, freezing Alvin with its milky stare. He thought about running back into the bedroom and hiding in the closet but knew he wouldn't do that. How long would he be stuck there if he did? He didn't know. How many more rades, smelling fresh meat, would show up while he was in there? Would they hurt the elderly couple sleeping in the bed? Alvin didn't want to put them at risk. At least they were alive, somewhere, while he walked this purgatory.

The rade began walking toward him, smooth and glowing, ominously long needle fingernails extending down past its knee.

Then Alvin didn't know if he wanted to move. He imagined those needles sliding into him. He almost longed for it. He felt all the throbbing wounds over his body, tasted the blood and vomit on the back of his tongue. All those needles could make the discomfort go away. He straightened up and faced the rade. He was ready to give himself to it.

There was a flash and a loud explosion. The rade's head burst in a green corona. The fetid stink of a sewer filled the room. Alvin would have vomited if he'd had anything left.

He looked to his left. Benjamin Teats stood in the doorway of the house holding a shotgun against his shoulder.

"Courtesy of the police," he said.

"Ben!" Alvin was glad to see him.

The headless rade took a couple staggering steps to the side before collapsing onto the carpet, oozing stinking green fluid.

"It took you forever to find this place," Ben said. "I

guess I overestimated your intelligence."

"I got sidetracked. I think I found it by chance." Even with the shirt, Alvin was still freezing. He wrapped his arms around himself.

"I've come here five times waiting for you."

"I've only been out of the station for a day, at most. Besides, I thought you weren't going to leave your cell?"

"I was just waiting for the right person to leave it for. I know the secret so I can leave it whenever I want."

"Did you bash your head against the bars too?"

"No. I have the keys." He held up a key ring and jangled them.

Alvin drew closer to him until he remembered his putrid smell.

"So," Ben said, "I trust you have a plan?"

"I don't know what I'm doing, Ben. The demolition crew is up on my house. They could detonate it at any time. I need to get to the Point so I can file some papers and make them stop. I need to get to my house and make sure they haven't blown it up yet. I feel sick. Everyone's turning to rust. Am I turning to rust, Ben? Is that what happens to people when they go to sleep? Is it the rust that makes them go to sleep in the first place? We need to go. We need to get out of here. We need to go. We need to go by my house. Can you take me by my house, Ben?"

"Relax," Ben said. "I got us a car from the station, too. We'll be able to make good time. We can cruise by your house and see how far along they are. Then I have something I need to do. Then we can go to the Point but, I have to tell you, if you don't have any ID or anything and you're not the only one who owns the house, it's almost impossible to get them to reverse a decision."

"But they *have* to. They can't just blow up the house. Where will I go? What'll happen to April?"

"They hardly ever detonate houses at night."

"I thought you said it was always night."

"And they like to detonate houses at the crack of dawn."

"When is dawn? It has to be close. It's been night for so long. I can't remember the last time I saw the sun. What was it you had to do?"

"I have to settle a score. It'll be quick. I promise."

"Can't you just take me to the Point?"

"No. I need your help."

"Then you need to tell me what it is we're doing."

"I have to find out what happened to Lars. I have to know what happens to those people. Is that good enough for you?"

"Why?"

"Because I have to find out if life is worth living or not. If I think what happens to those people is really what happens to those people, then I'm not so sure I need to continue living. But I'll need someone to keep an eye out. Maybe create a distraction."

"Let's go. We have to be quick."

They went outside and a blast of cold air hit Alvin as they began walking toward the cruiser. He looked up at the night sky. White flakes drifted down from it.

"Is it snowing?" Alvin asked.

"No. That's just some shit that comes from the Point. That's how they clean out their smokestacks. They just blow everything into the sky."

"It's still kind of pretty." Alvin watched the white flakes fluttering through the night sky, settling on the dirty houses and vacant lots and ruins of detonated houses. A dog howled sickly in the distance. Alvin and Ben got into the car. Alvin shivered so hard his teeth were chattering.

Ben pulled away from the curb. "No offense but you look like shit."

"I've had a rough time. Archer was trying to assassinate me."

"Oh, Archer. He was another good reason to stay in prison. You know, he's famous for hunting rades but he hunts humans as well. You're not the first."

"I think I killed him."

Ben looked momentarily stunned. "Hm."

Ben gunned the car and nailed a rade. It got caught under the car and Alvin watched the glowing trail of green from the side mirror until the rade dislodged and went tumbling limply along the asphalt. Ben stopped at a red light and Alvin looked to his right. A skinny dog was humping the mangled corpse, bones visible, of another dog. Behind them, a dilapidated house loomed.

Alvin poked his tongue, rolled down the window, and dry heaved out of it. A horrible stink wafted from the dead dog. The living dog caught the cruiser out of the corner of his eye and started growling.

The light was still red.

"Jesus Christ." Alvin wiped his lips with the back of his hand. "Can we get the fuck out of here?"

Alvin's voice snapped Ben out of a fog. "Oh, sorry." He jammed the accelerator and they went speeding up Payne, diving into and skidding around an elaborate series of alleyways, before ending up in front of Alvin's house.

"Looks like they're still up there," Ben said.

The house was now completely covered in the multicolored wire, even the windows. Were April and his simulacrum in there? He imagined them fucking. He imagined April on her hands and knees while the simulacrum plugged her from behind. He imagined her barking out in furious ecstasy. He imagined her getting pregnant. He imagined her happy. He imagined both of them happy with a child.

He couldn't give her that.

That was what he needed to get back into the house. He shook the thought away. That was ridiculous. He couldn't just give her a baby.

He rolled the window down and leaned out.

"I'm going to the Point to fill out some paperwork!" he yelled. "You'd better not blow up my goddamn house! It's a mistake! You blow up my house and there's going to be hell to pay!"

A number of the workers moved to edge of the roof closest to him. He didn't like these men in their black jumpsuits and gas masks. Why did they need gas masks anyway? They were acting like his house was toxic. The white flakes were still fluttering from the black sky. The worker in the center of the group faced Alvin, put his hands together in front of him, and made motions like he was plunging a detonator.

"You're not going to get anywhere," Ben said. "We might as well go. We're just wasting time."

Alvin tried to spit at the workers but there wasn't any saliva in his mouth, only blood, and he wretched violently. Ben pulled away and Alvin rolled up the window to try and keep the cold air away from him.

A Hospital at Night
Part Ten

The shadow tapped gently on the doorframe. Mirabel stood up and walked toward it.

"Are you Ms. Blue?"

Mirabel shook her head and motioned toward April, who was still seated. "I'll just hop out for a sec," she said and disappeared into the ocean of fluorescence.

"Ms. Blue. I'm Detective Wilson Fouquette. Wilson. Do you mind if I close this?"

"Go ahead." April had a hard time making the words come out of her mouth. They wanted to get stuck in her scratchy throat.

The man shut the door. He wore a suit but she couldn't tell if it was black or blue or brown.

"Do you mind if I turn a light on?"

"Go ahead."

He turned the light on and it stung April's eyes. He was tall and slender with short black hair and an angular face. He carried a bunch of flowers in his right hand. He sat them on the table beside Alvin's bed.

He came to sit down next to her and April had the feeling she was locked in a room with a rapist or a vampire. Then she looked at Alvin and thought maybe he was the vampire.

Ten

Ben ran the car up onto the curb in front of the station. Alvin felt numb and distant. Two rades were in front of the door to the station.

"Get out," Ben said.

Alvin stepped out of the car. It felt so cold. He felt like his skin was drawn too tightly around his muscles and bones. He wanted to find someplace warm and lie down. Ben crossed to the back of the cruiser and pulled the trunk open.

"Dammit," Ben said. "I thought there would be some heavy equipment back here."

Alvin wandered to the trunk of the car, keeping his arms wrapped tightly around himself. "What do you mean?"

"Guns. Tear gas. Weapons."

"Ben, what are you doing?"

"Correcting crimes against humanity."

Alvin wanted to say it didn't make any sense. He wanted to say it wasn't a good idea. But the more he thought about it, the more it *did* make sense. Everyone in the police station was crooked. Dayton had fallen into ruins. They had given complete control to the Point and now you had women having sex with people so they could get pregnant and sell the abortions, demolition crews blowing up houses, simulacra taking the place of real people, sociopaths like Archer running around, dangerous rades that were seen as something little more than sport. It was easy to see how Ben blamed them for everything. Besides, they had locked him up for doing nothing at all. In fact, he had escaped only a while ago. He shouldn't even be here. Why did he let Ben take him here? It was hard to find a reason. It was hard to focus on what was even happening in front of him. He just knew he had to get to the Point. And then he thought, maybe, if that's where they really take all the abortions, he could get a baby at the Point. Maybe some of them weren't dead yet. Maybe the Point did the same thing with children as it did with some of their parents—snatch them up and replace them with another version.

Ben was quicker than Alvin thought he would be. He began walking toward the station, toward the rades. Alvin tried to cross to the driver's side of the car. He was going to hop in and take it to the Point. But it was hard to move. His skeleton felt leaden. His muscles felt like wet paper towels.

"Alvin, I'll need you to help." Ben was now beside him, grabbing him by an arm and dragging him toward the rades. And again, Alvin felt that urge to just lie down and let them swarm him with their needle fingers.

Ben let go of Alvin about halfway to the station and continued moving toward the rades.

They moved to attack Ben and he became a blur of fists and legs, his dirty overcoat flapping around him. Maybe he had the weapon of stink. Alvin began moving toward them, toward the station. If he could at least get the doors open while Ben fought the rades... Ben had knocked one of them down the stairs and Alvin moved around it, feeling more like he was swimming. He reached the doors and grabbed the vertical industrial handle.

The remaining rade stabbed his sharp-fingered hand toward Ben. Ben threw out his left arm, absorbing the blow with a popping of skin, and took a wild swing with his right hand. The rade's head disintegrated with a spray of green before it collapsed on the steps with the rest of them.

Alvin swung the door open. Ben ran inside and Alvin followed, pulling the door shut.

"Lock it," Ben said.

Alvin did, slowly and clumsily.

The station was alive with vice.

To Alvin's left, an officer was 69ing with a woman, his pants and belt down around his ankles. Alvin grabbed the gun from the holster before the officer had time to stop, before even he himself knew what he was doing. Ben, being more familiar with the station, disappeared into a room on the far side.

As more of the officers realized what was happening, they stopped their fornicating and turned toward Alvin. Some then pulled up their pants and some of them kicked them off completely.

"Stop right there," an Officer Cuntbanger announced.

The girl who he had been servicing bent down in front of him and backed herself onto his penis. Alvin noticed the same thing happening all around the station. The officers stopping their sex acts and paying attention to him while the women, probably abortion whores, fastened themselves on and continued gyrating.

He also noticed a lot of weapons pointed at him.

Morning is Dead

Come on, Ben. Where the hell are you?

The office of the station exploded in a deafening roar. Alvin fell behind a desk, not knowing if that would do a lot of good, thinking he probably wouldn't feel anything anyway and maybe what he would feel would be better than how he felt now. He put his back to the noise, drew his knees up to his chest, squeezed his eyes shut, and put his fingers in his ears. He sat there and shivered, all of his muscles drawn tight, his brain racing around in circles. The smell of cordite, blood, shit, and fear assaulted his nostrils. Less than a minute later, the horrible sound stopped.

Machine gun fire, he thought, although he wasn't sure. Other than movies, he didn't think he'd ever heard machine gun fire. The movies were nowhere near as loud and terrible as what he had just heard, even through whatever gauzy cocoon he was in.

"Alvin!" Ben called.

Slowly, Alvin stood up from behind the desk and fought the dizzying desire to collapse again. The office was awash with carnage. Several of the girls were still in the process of scrambling for the front door, adjusting their clothes as they went. Eyes widening, Alvin surveyed the violence of the room—officers' heads pulped, limbs severed and twitching on the floor, a couple of bodies completely cut in half—until his eyes came to rest on Ben, standing at the far side of the office, smoking assault rifles in either hand.

"Ben?" Alvin couldn't even hear himself over the ringing in his ears.

"I knew where they kept the heavy artillery. It made things a lot easier."

"Did you have to kill them all?"

"I don't think they were doing anyone any favors. I'm

just righting some wrongs. I still need to find the Processor."

Ben turned to walk down the long hall in front of the prison cells. They were empty at the moment. Alvin followed, stepping through the congealing blood on the floor. He looked down at the service revolver in his hand and wondered if he would even need it. Probably not with Ben around.

Ben reached the Processor's door before Alvin. He tugged at the knob.

"It's locked," he said.

"What?" Alvin still had trouble hearing.

"It's locked! Stay back!"

Alvin stopped where he was. Ben took a step back from it, leveled the assault rifle and fired off a couple rounds. The wood around the handle shredded, the door swinging inward. Ben motioned for Alvin to follow him.

Alvin entered the mostly empty room and stood next to Ben.

"She's gone," Alvin said.

"She didn't leave by the front door. There aren't many places she could go. I have to take care of something first."

Ben crouched and placed the assault rifles on the floor. He pulled up his sleeve to reveal four large green knots.

"Is that where...?"

"The rade got me? Yeah. You have to drain them before the toxin can get through your body."

He squeezed the first of the knots. It grew tight against the skin, the flesh surrounding it a bright red, before bursting. Ben turned his arm over to let the poison drip to the floor.

"Anything I can do to help?" Alvin looked at the spilled

fluid and licked his sandpaper lips. He had the sudden urge to drop onto his knees and lap it up.

"Just be patient. I have to make sure these are drained as best as possible or I might end up losing the arm."

"Damn. I'm sorry, Ben. I should have been there helping you."

"Nothing you could have done. At least you're alive."

"There is that." Alvin walked around the room. In the corner was a stack of large envelopes, the plastic kind. Alvin picked up the top one. It felt padded and heavier than it looked.

The address said:

THE POINT
RE: LARS KRALL
DAYTON OH 45402

The return address said simply:

STATION 652

"Ben? You know what these are?"

Ben glanced over. All the wounds were now open, dribbling their battery acid stink all over the floor. "Those are Lars."

"Why would Lars get this much mail?"

"No. They *are* Lars. Those envelopes are filled with his flesh, waiting to be transported to the Point."

"Like the abortions."

"Exactly. To make more simulacra."

Alvin licked his lips. He looked at the envelopes. He looked at the pool of toxin on the floor. He thought about the Point. He tried not to feel nauseous. If he threw up he was afraid his insides would come out and consume the outside of his body.

Ben pulled a gross-looking handkerchief from his coat pocket and pressed it to his wounds before tying it around his arm. "Okay, ready to go."

Ben walked toward the back of the room, under the surveillance camera mounted on the wall. The wall swung inward, opening into blackness.

"Bitch cut the lights," Ben said. "Shut the door behind you. We're going to be going down some stairs and then opening another door. She'll probably try and use the element of surprise to get by us. Grab her if you can. Don't let her get by or she's gone. Got it?"

"I don't think I can stop anything, Ben."

"Do you think you can throw yourself in front of her?"

"I guess."

"Good enough."

Ben stopped at the bottom of the stairs. Alvin nearly ran into him.

"Like I said," Ben whispered. "She'll probably be waiting by the door. I'll open it a crack and you run through it. Knock her back if you can. I'll come in right behind you and guard the door. Ready?"

Alvin wasn't but, then again, he never would be. "Sure," he said.

"On three.

"One.

"Two.

"Three!"

The door opened a crack. Light burst through but Alvin had already committed. He stumbled and fell forward, blinded by all the light but keeping his hand planted on his gun.

The door slammed shut behind him.

A lock was turned.

He heard the Processor say, "Good work."

Anger and confusion clouded the rest of his immediate thoughts.

With his gun in his right hand, he shielded the light with his left. Slowly, things came into focus. At first, it was hard for him to believe what he saw but then he cursed himself for being so stupid. Of course he had trusted Ben. After helping him escape, he would have believed anything Ben said. But that was exactly what Ben wanted, wasn't it? And he didn't really help him escape anything. Just led him back to the beginning. Not funny.

"Ben?"

"I'm sorry, Alvin."

"No you're not. This is exactly what you wanted."

"Well... yeah."

The Processor took a step toward Alvin. Her gnarled hand hung down to her knees. He imagined the rotting meat caught under the nails. He wondered if she ripped people like Lars apart with her hand. People like Lars? Hell, *he* was people like Lars. He guessed he would find out how she did it soon enough.

"Just tell me why," he asked Ben, trying to ignore the Processor.

"Money. Isn't that why anyone does anything?"

"But you killed all the officers."

"Did I? I don't think anyone will believe that. I think, maybe, *you* killed the officers."

Alvin scanned the brightly lighted room around him. It

looked a lot like Archer's Shucking Room. Only this one was used to shuck humans, not rades.

Alvin took a deep breath. It felt like breathing in all that sterile fluorescent light. It entered his lungs and crackled along his bones. He didn't feel so tired anymore. He felt like something wanted him to move. He shook a little more violently and imagined wires hanging from the ceiling, maybe hanging from the sky, into him, into his muscles. They could yank him whatever way they wanted him to go.

"You're crazier than Archer," Alvin said.

Ben threw back his head and laughed.

The strings tried to jerk him up but he wanted to lie on the floor and figure out how he was going to get to the Point. How he was going to get out of here.

The Processor had a murderous hand that Alvin thought he could outrun. Ben had an assault rifle in each hand that he was pretty sure he could not outrun.

He couldn't think anymore. His arm jerked up and he aimed his gun at Ben and fired as many times as he could. Ben shot back but he was probably already dead and the shots went all over the place. Thankfully, none of them went into Alvin.

He charged for the door, slammed into it and frantically tried the knob.

The Processor's hand slashed at his back, parting flesh.

Alvin screamed with pain and yanked the door back into the room. He turned and fired about where he thought the Processor should be, darted through the door, and let it bang back into the frame. He ran up the dark stairs and into the office of the station, nearly slipping in all the blood. He dropped his gun, wished he knew where they kept the assault rifles, and settled for another pistol in a dead cop's belt.

Casting quick glances behind himself, Alvin continued outside. He expected it to be alive with rades but the only things out there were human—officers' concubines and many more women and girls.

A trashy-looking girl with bleached blond hair, too much make-up, wearing skin tight pants and something that looked more like a bra than a shirt said, "Why'd you have to kill all our fucks. Now how we gonna get pregnant?"

"Don't matter anyway," another girl said, approaching from across the street. "Dr. Lucky shut down. Said he needs to rest."

"He ain't never done that before."

"I always thought there was two of 'em."

"What do we do now?"

"I don't know. Things are really weird."

Alvin was aware that he was the only male within eye-shot and he wondered how many of them were eager to conceive.

"The station is filled with booze and drugs," he said and took off running for his car, jerked by those puppet strings, moving without feeling anything.

Where were all the rades? He expected to see them swarming his car, at least.

He unlocked the door and slid behind the wheel.

A Hospital at Night
Part Eleven

Detective Fouquette, Wilson, raked a big, bony hand across his face. He looked tired. April glanced toward him and then at the figure in the bed. Everything now seemed so clean and exposed. This was an examination, she was sure. The part where everything would be thrown open and laid bare.

"First of all, let me say this isn't a formal questioning," Wilson said. "I'm here on my own, not as part of the investigation. That might come later."

"Might?"

"Probably depending on whether or not Mr. Blue lives. If he dies, I'm sure there will be some questions, but if he happens to live, it'll be drawn out indefinitely, I'm sure."

April nodded.

"Because you were harmed and Doctor Morning is now dead, I feel somewhat apologetic. I know you're aware of how Mr. Blue ended up in his current condition and how Dr. Morning died. I felt as though I should fill you in on the events leading up to that. I'm still a little lost, trying to piece it all together, and that's where I was hoping you could help me."

"I'll tell you what I can."

"Very well." Wilson sat up straight in the chair and produced a notebook from the inside of his black blazer. He began reading in a staccato fashion.

Eleven

To get to the Point, Alvin had to drive through downtown. He turned the radio to his favorite station but the only thing it picked up was static. He wasn't surprised.

The car had a quarter tank of gas. He didn't know what it was he expected to see. What he saw was more of the same. Darkened buildings, some of them demolished. Darkened streets. A few scattered people wandering aimlessly. A lot more women than men.

He wondered how long it would take for people to realize what had happened at the police station. He wondered if it would be difficult to get into the Point. He wondered if he would be able to fill out the necessary paperwork to stop the detonation of his house. He wondered if he needed to think about anything since what his body did now seemed completely out of control.

A light in front of him turned red. He planned on blowing right through it. If there were still any cruisers on the road, he knew they were probably headed back to the station. But he depressed the brake anyway, and the car rolled to a stop. He felt like he could struggle to press the accelerator but knew he would only be opposing some other force. The thought of it made him exhausted.

The passenger door opened and someone flung himself into the seat.

Alvin panicked and yelped.

The first thing he thought about was jumping back out of the car and running. The next thing he thought about was the gun, but his unwelcome visitor now sat upon the gun. Then he thought about who his unwelcome visitor was.

Alvin stared at him, unbelieving.

The burns were a pretty good indicator.

"I'm charred. You can stop staring."

But Alvin couldn't stop staring. He didn't know how this person was alive. The left half of his head was blackened tissue and raw red pulp over charred skull and teeth. The hair on his right side was fried, sticking out wildly toward the window. His clothes were melted to his body. He was missing a foot, white bone sticking out of the blackened meat. His bombs were strapped across his body, crisscrossing his chest like bandoleers.

"We need to get moving."

"How are you still alive?"

"How are you still an asshole? Come on. Chop chop." Archer tapped the dashboard.

"To the Point?"

"Where else?"

"Are you going to blow it up?"

"Hell yeah I'm going to blow it up."

"I need to fill out some papers first."

"It won't do you any good."

Alvin's foot lifted from the brake and pressed the accelerator. Archer had found the gun and now held it pointed on Alvin. Alvin hoped his body did what it was supposed to do. Maybe if Archer blew up the Point, then the demolition crew would have to stop. If the very orders that told them to do what they were doing no longer existed, then why follow through with it? Archer only had one good leg and most of his body was burned. Alvin thought he could probably beat him into the Point, with his only restraint being the wires that guided him. He guessed, in the end, he would do what his body wanted him to do.

A Hospital at Night
Part Twelve

At 9:04, her estranged husband, Alvin Blue was arrested and held in a cell.

The last time he appeared on the surveillance film was at 10:16.

After that, it appeared the cell was empty yet Alvin was never released.

At 12:36 PM, two heavily armed assailants opened fire on the police station, killing everyone in uniform.

"The underlying motive seemed to be drugs. It is believed the station was either holding a potential informant, gang rival, or it's even possible that the assailants, out of their heads, were raiding the station's evidence room for narcotics.

"Surveillance footage shows one man leaving the station. It is believed that man is your estranged husband, Alvin Blue. Preliminary examination of the crime scene has not found the remains of the remaining suspect. The suspect is thought to be a man named Brian Tippin."

Twelve

Leaving downtown behind, they drove through a dilapidated suburb that seemed to exist to feed the Point. The houses were shrunken and drained of color. Archer filled the car with a powerful reek. The strength of it reminded Alvin of Ben but this stink was different, even closer to death. He wanted to roll down the window but he couldn't move his arm. They crested a hill and the Point lay towering above them on the next hill, huge and black against the night sky, like something more science fiction than reality, giant smoke stacks billowing steam and fire. Here, even over Archer's stench, he could smell the gaseous reek of the Point.

They made their way up the hill. The gate in front of them was closed but it was only a tall chain link fence and the car drove through it. Archer nodded greedily in the passenger seat, as though this were exactly what he wanted Alvin to do.

Could Archer be the one pulling his marionette strings? Could he now be completely under Archer's power? Did Archer have that kind of power?

Once they were in the parking lot, Alvin's foot jammed on the brakes and the car screeched to a halt.

"No," Archer said. "You're supposed to drive into it. Right into the administration building."

Alvin threw open the door and jerked his way out of the car. He took off running toward the Point. He heard Archer's gun crack behind him but if any of the bullets hit him, he didn't feel a thing. Archer screamed something behind him but Alvin didn't care what it was.

He continued to charge toward the Point, those sky wires jerking him along so he felt like he was barely even touching the ground. To his right, at one of the loading docks, he saw a cargo truck with "Dr. Lucky's" stenciled across the side. Under the words was a baby's head. The baby had dollar signs for eyes.

Alvin reached the threshold of the Point and it felt like something cut the wires propelling him forward. His knees buckled and he tumbled to the ground.

He had come in one of the large bay doors of the foundry. They usually kept these open so the heat didn't build up. Alvin stood up and surveyed this section of the Point.

It wasn't the Point he remembered.

A lot of the equipment was still here but it was all covered in rust. Everything was covered in rust. It dropped in flakes from the ceiling, several stories above him. It coated the ground and crunched under his feet. There wasn't anyone working. Off to his right, where Dr. Lucky's truck was parked for unloading, he saw fetuses piled twenty feet into the air. Some of them looked red and some of them looked purple and some of them were flesh colored. Umbilical cords trailed from some of them while others didn't resemble much of anything at all.

Some of them were moving.

Alvin dropped to his knees and vomited. He thought it would be more dry heaves. Rust flowed from his mouth.

No, Alvin thought. He hadn't been asleep. He couldn't be rusting.

He vomited more rust. He could feel it on his tongue, running down his throat. He could feel it sitting in his stomach. Rust. Rotten metal.

There wasn't any paperwork to fill out here. He knew he could search the entire Point—even the administration building—and he wouldn't find anything but rust and more rust.

He walked toward the pile of fetuses, moving closer and closer. He could hear some of them crying. He felt like an old woman staring at a pile of fruit. Or a vulture. He picked one of the moving ones up. It had its eyes closed. It was a boy. Alvin had to reach down and pry its eyes open to make sure it wasn't filled with rust. He pulled it close to his chest and bolted out of the Point.

Outside, Archer nearly plowed into him with the car. Alvin turned to watch him pass. He could hear Archer laughing from inside the car. Alvin began running toward town, toward home. He heard a giant explosion behind him and felt the heat on his back.

A Hospital at Night
Part Thirteen

At 1:14 AM, someone bombed the Point. According to surveillance footage, it was believed Alvin was a part of this as well. The other individual in the car was believed to be a man named John Strange.

"It doesn't make any sense. I can't make the connection between a plot to bomb the Point and a small time drug cartel. It would appear that Alvin was a pawn in both of these crimes.

"Something else. A woman who Alvin was believed to be having sexual relations with was found dead outside her apartment earlier this evening.

"Ms. Blue, what would make your husband go on a killing spree of this magnitude?"

"I don't think I can answer any questions right now."

She could barely talk. It was something she didn't want to know. It was something she couldn't take responsibility for. She knew if she had scratched the surface she would have found a lonely, unstable man. Possibly a drug addict. Possibly unstable because of the drugs. But this was so much worse. This was like scratching the surface to have the insides blow up in her face.

"That's very well, Ms. Blue. As I said before, this is not a formal examination. I understand your husband had been estranged for quite a while and this all may come as as much of a surprise to you as it does to me. I just wanted to prepare you for some of what you will have to go through should Mr. Blue make it through this. I lost a lot of friends tonight, Ms. Blue, and I can assure you, mentally ill or not, Mr. Blue will not be alive for very long if he does wake up. There will be questioning and a trial, sure, but I have friends in every facet of the system and, again, I can assure you, if he wakes up he has joined the ranks of the living dead."

April nodded. She was crying again. And trying to digest what Wilson was telling her. Was he threatening her? Or urging her?

He stood up and patted her on the shoulder. "I just don't want anyone else to suffer more than they have to."

And then he was gone, flipping the lights off on his way out, bringing the night inside the hospital room.

Thirteen

Alvin ran on the outskirts of the city. The night came alive with sirens but it sounded like they were very far away, on the other side of the earth. He kept the baby pressed to his chest. The heaviness that had infested him, the feeling that all of his bones were made out of heavy metal had returned. As he ran, all of his wounds opened up—his forehead, his cheek, his back, his arm, his hand—and he could feel rust pouring out of them. He felt like the harder he ran the lighter he became. Now he just wanted to get back home. He thought if he could make it home before the demolition crew blew it up, then he could show April the baby, and then she would be happy and then it wouldn't matter if they blew the house up or not because they could be happy anywhere.

Rades skulked the streets as Alvin passed by several alleys, but they couldn't move fast enough to catch him. They probably sensed the rust anyway. He was no longer of any use to them.

He turned onto his street. Everything felt different. He heard birds chirping, heralding the beginning of morning.

The air felt lighter and less oppressive. Everything glistened with dew. Even the ruined houses seemed to hold promise, like flowers or trees could spring from them.

The demolition crew stood in the middle of his road. They had a large detonator in front of them.

Alvin could see his house. It was completely covered in wires. A twist of wires, all bright colors—red and green and yellow—snaked from the house to the detonator.

Alvin charged up onto his lawn, moving toward the house.

"April! April!" he called.

Above the house, just over the roof, he thought he could see a trace of dawn limning the sky.

He held the baby out in front of him.

A Hospital at Night
Part Fourteen

The night hugged April. She stood above Alvin but all she saw was gauze and tubes. She already knew more about him than she ever wanted to. She wanted to remember him the way he had been when they got married—before the drugs or the insanity or the boredom. She didn't want to think about him throwing a homemade bomb through the window. She didn't want to think about him throwing himself into the flames. She didn't want to wonder if he was doing it to save her or kill himself. She didn't want to see him become a criminal. She didn't want to see him become a prisoner. And she didn't want to spend the rest of her life under the same scrutiny. She pulled on a pair of latex gloves. She positioned her hands around Alvin's neck and paused to make sure she couldn't hear any footsteps out in the hall, to make sure Mirabel wasn't coming back to check on her, to make sure the detective wasn't going to come back and ask her any more questions.

Her insides were screaming but everything around her was silent. She couldn't even hear any sounds coming from outside. The only thing she could hear was the beeping of the heart monitor and a cacophony of voices in her head.

She would never know if this was the right thing to do. She just had to figure out if she could live with herself if she did it. No one was going to tell her it was right or wrong. No one was going to tell her what she should do. If that voice existed, if there was someone who could help her navigate her life, surely they would have intervened a long time ago.

Beep. Beep. Beep.

Alvin opened his eyes.

April squeezed.

Fourteen

Holding the baby out in front of him, he looked at the sky over the house, wanting to see a shred of sunlight. He looked at the house, wanting to see April.

He heard the demolition crew behind him breathing. Maybe they were laughing. He thought he could see April in front of him. Her face looked huge. As big as the sky. Then he heard the dull click of the detonator being depressed and he felt all the rust inside of him press its way out through his skin like sweat. He searched his hands for the baby but the only thing he held was fire and then he couldn't even see his hands as everything fragmented into flakes of rust and fragmented further into dust and—

A Hospital at Night
Part Fifteen

April left Alvin's room and went to the nurse's station.

"I think he's gone."

Mirabel, all business, stood up quickly, paging the doctor and heading to Alvin's room.

April grabbed Mirabel's keys, held on a bright orange, coiled band, and walked to the elevator. She took the elevator to the top floor, the psych ward. Then she found the stairwell that led to the roof. She unlocked it and climbed the stairs. She went out onto the roof. She moved to the edge.

She looked out over the city. It wasn't so bad here. There were trees and nice houses. The birds were chirping. The air was cool and moist. Refreshing. But she thought about what could be happening in the darkest parts of the city and on the outskirts of the city. She wanted the sun to blast its way through the clouds and shine down on everything, drive all the badness into the soil like a cockroach.

She thought about how easy it would be to just keep moving right off the roof. She was high enough up. And perhaps she would have if it was just her. But it wasn't. Not anymore. She knew the baby was Brett's and she also knew that that was not the only reason they were together. It was just something that happened. She was in pieces. She knew that. But they were pieces that could, with time, be stitched together. If she let herself plunge from the roof she knew there would be no mending that.

She took in a deep breath.

Someone had left an old lawn chair up here, probably one of the janitors. Maybe this was where he took his lunch break. April pulled the chair over to the ledge and sat down. She put her feet up and waited for the morning sun.

Email this guy at andersenprunty@yahoo.com. Visit him on the web at www.andersenprunty.com.